THE SHOCK OF JOE'S LIFE

The Hardys circled around to the front of the house and found the Gray Man with his gun drawn, standing over two men lying facedown on the ground, hands clasped over their heads.

"There were four of them," the Gray Man said. "I managed to stop these two, but the other two got away."

A chill ran down Joe's spine. "Got away? Where did they go?"

"I don't know," the Gray Man answered. "I was sort of busy at the time. Find some rope so we can tie up these scum."

Joe didn't hear him because he had bolted across the field and into the woods, his heart pounding frantically. He skidded to a halt when he realized the van was gone. Joe's heart sank. The terrorists had stolen his van—and kidnapped Vanessa....

Books in THE HARDY BOYS CASEFILES™ Series

Available from ARCHWAY Paperbacks

THE HARDY BOYS CASEFILES NO. 100

TRUE THRILLER

FRANKLIN W. DIXON

AN ARCHWAY PAPERBACK
Published by POCKET BOOKS
New York   London   Toronto   Sydney   Tokyo   Singapore

AN ARCHWAY PAPERBACK *Original*

 An Archway Paperback published by
POCKET BOOKS, a division of Simon & Schuster Inc.
1230 Avenue of the Americas, New York, NY 10020

ISBN: 0-671-88211-2

First Archway Paperback printing June 1995

10 9 8 7 6 5 4 3 2 1

THE HARDY BOYS, AN ARCHWAY PAPERBACK and colophon are registered trademarks of Simon & Schuster Inc.

THE HARDY BOYS CASEFILES is a trademark of Simon & Schuster Inc.

Cover art by Brian Kotzky

Printed in the U.S.A.

IL 6+

TRUE THRILLER

Chapter
1

"SHH!" JOE HARDY HISSED, shooting a sharp glance at his brother. "I'm trying to concentrate. This is my last shot. I have to make it count."

Frank grinned and turned to his girlfriend, Callie Shaw, raising a finger to his lips. Callie rolled her eyes at Joe's girlfriend, Vanessa Bender, who shrugged and smiled.

Joe's cool blue eyes shifted back to the sights on the bow. He adjusted his left arm slightly to center the target in the crosshairs, took a slow, deep breath, and fired.

The bow made a soft metallic twang and sent a jolt through Joe's arm as if he'd whacked a sledgehammer through pavement.

Joe watched intently as his shot hit the target

with deadly force. The shaft of the arrow was embedded in the red circle—just outside the yellow bull's-eye.

Joe groaned as he handed the bow to Vanessa. "Okay," he conceded, "you win."

"You're not really surprised, are you?" she asked as they walked across the field toward the target, which was propped against a stand in the middle of a field behind the old farmhouse where she lived. "I told you I've been practicing almost every day."

"I know," Joe said. "I just thought—"

"He just thought he'd win because he's a guy!" Callie called out.

Joe twisted his head around and scowled at Callie. She responded with a smug grin. When Joe turned back to Vanessa and caught the twinkle in her blue-green eyes, he smiled sheepishly. He helped her pluck the arrows out of the target, and then they trudged back across the overgrown field.

"Are you really serious about trying out for the Olympics?" Frank asked Vanessa when she returned.

"Why not?" Vanessa answered, standing behind a line that marked off the regulation seventy meters from the target. "If I train hard for the next two years, I might have a chance of making the team."

She nocked a steel-tipped arrow into the bow,

drew back the string, squinted down the sight, and let the arrow fly. The arrow thunked into the target, slightly off dead center but solidly in the yellow bull's-eye zone.

"It would take me a couple of years just to figure out how that thing works," Joe said, eyeing the weapon in Vanessa's hand.

The bowstring was a sturdy metal cable, and the bow itself was a combination of two curved metal "limbs" bolted to a molded fiberglass stock that had a contoured handgrip, a crosshair sight, and a gadget that resembled a gun silencer, jutting out in front.

Vanessa had explained that the foot-long narrow cylinder was a hydraulic stabilizer that improved accuracy by absorbing some of the bow stock. Joe hadn't really understood the need for the shock-absorbing gizmo until the first time he felt the jolt shoot up his arm when he released the bowstring and sent an arrow streaking toward the target.

Vanessa fired off twelve arrows in rapid succession. Eight of them hit the yellow bull's-eye. Three punctured the red circle just outside the center, and one landed in the blue concentric circle that bordered the red.

"With a little more practice, you'll be hitting the bull's-eye every time," Joe said.

"It'll take more than practice," Vanessa said as they retrieved the arrows and gathered up the rest of the gear. "I need to start a weight-training program to build up my upper-body strength."

Frank and Callie focused on Joe, waiting to see how he would react to the news that his girlfriend was about to become a weight lifter. Joe decided to keep his mouth shut and his thoughts to himself.

The old farm that Vanessa's mother had converted into an animation studio and home was a fair distance outside of Bayport, where the Hardys lived. Joe was dreading the drive back to town because Vanessa wasn't the only one who had beaten him in the archery contest. Callie had outscored him by ten points, and Joe was sure she would gloat all the way home.

If Callie had intended to give Joe a hard time, she never got the chance, because the cellular phone in the Hardys' van rang almost as soon as Frank pulled out of Vanessa's driveway.

Joe picked up the portable phone and was greeted by a rapid burst of staccato speech. "I'm trying to contact Frank and Joe Hardy," a man said. "It's imperative that I talk to them."

"Start talking," Joe replied. "I'm Joe Hardy."

"At last!" the man said. "I've spent the past two weeks tracking you down."

Joe didn't like the sound of that. The Hardys had "tracked down" more than a few characters themselves—and most of them had ended up in jail. Joe racked his brain for anything he might have done that could have gotten him in trouble. All that came to mind was the book he had forgotten to return at the end of the school year, but he seriously doubted that the library police were hot on his trail.

"I don't suppose you're calling to tell me I won the state lottery," Joe ventured.

Joe heard a dry chuckle on the other end of the line. "I'm afraid not," the man said, "but I could make you very rich."

That got Joe's full attention. "Oh, really?" he said.

"Where are you now?" the man asked. "Can we meet?"

"Hold on a second," Joe said. "Who are you, and what do you want?"

"That's a long story," the man replied.

"Let's start with your name," Joe suggested. "That shouldn't take too long."

"Oh, I'm sorry," the man responded. "Let me introduce myself. "My name is—"

There was a sudden, high-pitched burst of static on the line. Joe jerked the phone away from his ear. "Yow!" he exclaimed, holding it at arm's length and rubbing his ear with his free hand. "That hurt!"

"What happened?" Callie asked.

"We just passed under some high-voltage power lines," Frank said. "All that raw current can generate powerful interference."

5

"Try the phone now," Frank suggested when they were well beyond the electric lines.

The shrill noise had faded, and Joe cautiously lifted the phone back up to his ear. "The line's dead," he said.

"Who was that?" Frank asked.

"I don't know," Joe answered. "The guy got cut off before he could tell me."

"Maybe he'll call back," Frank said.

"I hope so," Joe replied. "He said he could make us rich."

Frank rolled his eyes. "For a modest fee, no doubt. If he calls back and tries to convince you to invest your money in some get-rich-quick scheme, hang up."

Joe spread his hands and smiled. "No problem. I don't have any money."

"If you need us while we're away," Fenton Hardy said to his sons that night at dinner, "the number of our hotel in San Francisco is on the pad by the kitchen phone. I don't want to hear about problems after it's too late to do anything about them."

"They know what to do," Laura Hardy said, patting her husband's hand and smiling at him. "And it's not as if we'll be completely out of touch as Gertrude will be on her Caribbean cruise. The West Coast is only a phone call away."

"Oh, that reminds me," Frank and Joe's aunt Gertrude spoke up. Frank turned his attention to his aunt, who lived with them. "Some man called here two or three times today asking for you boys. He claimed it was urgent that he contact you as soon as possible. So I finally gave him your car phone number. I hope that was all right."

Joe looked up from his plate, losing interest in the peas he had lined up to spell his name. "What did the guy say?" Joe asked. "Did he leave a name or a return number?"

"No, he didn't," Gertrude Hardy said. "I'm sure he'll call back."

Fenton Hardy cleared his throat. "Let's get back on track here, okay? Since your mother and I will be at the conference and your aunt will be on a cruise, you two will have the house to yourselves for a full week. I'm not going to tell you how to behave—"

"So stop lecturing," Laura interrupted.

Fenton caught himself. "You're right. It's not like me to be nervous, but . . ." He glanced at his sister. "Are you sure you can't reschedule your cruise?"

"No, I can't," Gertrude Hardy said pleasantly but firmly. "Can a detective reschedule a crime or postpone the investigation until a more convenient time? This isn't an everyday cruise, you know," she continued. "There won't be another one like it until next year. Nothing in the world is going to keep me from my murder mystery cruise. A cab is picking me up tomorrow morning at six o'clock."

Frank and Joe exchanged a glance and a grin.

"We're counting on you to solve the murder and come home with the grand prize," Joe said. "The family honor is at stake."

"And I'm counting on you boys to hold down the fort while I'm away," Aunt Gertrude said.

Fenton Hardy seemed ready to add something, but the doorbell rang before he had a chance. It rang again a few seconds later, and the ringing was followed immediately by loud, insistent knocking.

"I'll get it," Joe volunteered. "Hold on," he called over the constant ringing and pounding. "I'm coming!"

Joe opened the door. A tall, skinny man with long brown hair thrust a package into his hands.

"What's this?" Joe asked.

The man consulted a pocket notebook. "Let's see—blond hair, blue eyes. You're Joe, right?"

"Is this for me?" Joe responded.

The man nodded.

"What is it?" Joe asked.

The man smiled. "It's a bomb."

Chapter

2

JOE FROZE. Part of his mind told him to clutch the package tightly and not move a muscle. Another part told him to throw the thing as far as he could, as fast as he could. Something else told him that both would probably lead to disaster. Too much pressure on the package might trigger the detonator. Any sudden movement might have the same effect.

"Frank!" he called out in a very calm manner so his mom or dad wouldn't come running. "Could you give me a hand here?"

Frank could see that something was wrong the second he stepped into the front hallway. Joe was standing stock-still, gripping a box wrapped in plain brown paper as if it contained the crown jewels of England or a live nuclear warhead.

A tall, lanky man with long brown hair and a diamond stud earring in his left ear also stood in the doorway, watching Joe intently.

"What's going on?" Frank asked.

"Call the bomb squad," Joe said. His voice was calm, but Frank could hear the underlying tension. "We have a serious situation here."

"What kind of situation?" Frank asked.

"The kind that involves stuff with a tendency to explode," Joe said evenly. "That's why I thought the bomb squad might be a good place to start."

"That won't be necessary," the long-haired man responded, plucking the package back from Joe in a single deft motion. "It's not really a bomb."

Frank watched as his brother's jaw dropped. Then Joe recovered. He reached out, grabbed the man by the front of his shirt, and lifted him into the air.

"What is this?" Joe growled. "And who are you?"

"Put me down and I'll tell you," the man gasped, his feet dancing several inches off the floor.

Frank put his hand on his brother's shoulder. "Give him a chance to explain. Then you can heave him out the door."

Joe glared at the man and let go of his shirt, sending him sprawling on the floor.

As the man got up, he tugged on his shirt and cleared his throat. "My name is Oliver Richards. I'm a writer. Maybe you've heard of me?" he asked expectantly.

Frank and Joe glanced at each other. Joe shrugged, and Frank shook his head. "Sorry. The name doesn't ring a bell."

Richards acted disappointed. "Well, ah, I'm a novelist. I write action-adventure thrillers."

"Do most writers of thrillers go around making bomb threats?" Joe snapped.

"That was a test," Richards explained. "I wanted to see how you'd react."

Joe frowned. "Why would you do a stupid thing like that?"

"Let me explain," Richards said. "I write fiction, but my stories are based on fact." He addressed both boys. "I've heard a lot about you two and the crimes you've solved. What I heard intrigued me, so I did a little digging. I even managed to get an interview with the Bayport police chief."

"Chief Collig?" Joe snorted. "I'll bet he had plenty to say about us, and not all good."

"He didn't say much," Richards cheerfully acknowledged. "And that's the way it should be. You have to fight the system—and the bad guys—to get any real justice in this world. Isn't that right?"

"Well, sure," Joe said in a hesitant tone, not really sure what Richards was talking about.

Richards smiled broadly. "You boys already have reputations, but I can make you *legends.*"

Frank and Joe exchanged a puzzled glance.

"I'm not sure I follow you," Frank said.

"It's really very simple," Richards continued. "I want to write a book about you and your crime-fighting adventures."

Joe stared at the writer, speechless.

"I know a lot about you," Richards said. "I always do heavy research on a subject before I write a single word, and I could write volumes about the stuff you've done. I couldn't dream up a better pair of heroes. You two are naturals—and you're real!"

"You want to write a book—about us?" Frank asked.

Richards nodded. "Just think of it," he said, a gleam in his eyes. "I could make you famous!"

"Do you really think so?" Joe responded, warming to the idea. He knew that a lot of best-sellers were made into blockbuster movies. He could already see himself on screen, striking a bold, heroic pose for the camera.

Frank glanced over at his brother. Where Joe saw fun and excitement, Frank usually saw trouble—and he was usually right. Frank saw trouble written all over Oliver Richards.

"It would be a fictionalized version, of course," Richards explained, "and we'd have to change your names to something like Hank and Moe Nardy—but your real-life adventures would be the core of the story. What do you think?"

"Moe Nardy?" Joe responded, raising an eyebrow.

"I'll come up with better names," Richards replied quickly.

"It certainly sounds like an interesting project," Fenton Hardy said from the background. "But you seem to know a lot more about my sons than we know about you."

Frank saw his father standing in the doorway between the hallway and the dining room.

"You say you're some kind of writer. . . ." Fenton's voice trailed off, with a hint of a question at the end. He gazed evenly at the stranger.

"Oliver Richards," the writer said, extending his hand and stepping over to Fenton.

"Do you have some identification I could see?" Fenton asked as the two men shook hands.

"Oh, sure," Richards replied, and reached for his wallet to slip out a business card.

Fenton studied the card. "You're a long way from Chicago, Mr. Richards."

Oliver Richards shrugged. "I go where the stories are."

Fenton smiled faintly and guided the writer toward the front door. "Are you staying anywhere in town where we can reach you?"

"Uh, yes, the Bayport Motel," Richards responded, his voice faltering as Fenton ushered him outside. "But I have a lot of ques—"

"I'm sure you do." Fenton cut him off smoothly. "And so do I. We'll be in touch." He swung the door closed in Richards's bewildered face and turned to his sons. "We don't know who that man really is or what he wants. Don't say another word to him until I have him checked out."

"No problem," Joe said. "He did most of the talking, anyway."

Frank caught the faraway expression in his brother's eyes and knew Joe was hoping Richards would turn out to be exactly what he claimed to be.

"Your mother and I don't have much time before we leave," Fenton Hardy said to Joe and Frank the next morning at breakfast. He took a sip of coffee, then added, "That writer couldn't have picked a worse time to show up."

"Did you find out anything about him?" Frank asked as he helped himself to another bagel.

Fenton sighed. "Not much. I pulled a few strings with some contacts, but I couldn't come up with a complete dossier on the guy. Richards appears to be legitimate," he said. "And that may be the best reason to stay away from him. I'm proud of both of you and you know that. But I wouldn't want to advertise your actions to the entire world."

Frank nodded. "I know what you mean. You can't be a very good detective if everybody knows who you are."

"I don't know," Joe countered. "Richards said he wouldn't use our real names. It might be fun."

Frank gave his brother a look. "Yeah, right— *Moe.*"

Just after a car horn honked outside, Laura Hardy walked into the kitchen. "The cab's here." She gave each of the boys a hug and a kiss.

"Have fun, Mom," Joe said.

"Yeah, have a great time," Frank said.

Fenton took a last sip of coffee and stood. "As far as this Richards character is concerned, my advice is to steer clear. In any case, be careful what you tell him."

"Hey," Joe responded. "Careful is my middle name."

Fenton Hardy focused on his younger son. "If it is, then you aren't Joe Hardy."

Joe grinned and shrugged. "Don't worry, Dad. We've handled a lot tougher characters than Richards."

"I know you have," Fenton said. "You always do—even when you probably shouldn't."

* * *

15

Joe enjoyed having the run of the house without his parents or aunt to check up on him. With school out for the summer, he was looking forward to a week of complete freedom, but he was soon reminded that freedom has a price. "Hey, Frank!" he called out late that afternoon as the sun started to set. "I'm getting hungry. What's for dinner?"

Frank poked his head out of his room, where he had been working on his computer. "I don't know. Mom said she left stuff in the freezer. It's your night to cook."

Joe gaped at his brother. "You mean you expect me to microwave something?"

Frank rolled his eyes. "I think even you can handle it."

The defrosting and cooking crisis was momentarily delayed by the ringing of the doorbell.

Joe ran to get it, followed by Frank. Oliver Richards was standing on the front porch when Joe opened the door.

"So, have you considered my offer?" Richards asked. "I've got some great ideas that will turn your life story into a best-seller. Maybe even a feature-length film."

"We like our life just the way it is," Frank remarked.

"Oh, come on," Richards cajoled. "At least let me buy you dinner and give me a chance to convince you."

16

Frank glanced at his brother, who was clearly swayed by the offer of a free meal. "Well, I guess it wouldn't hurt to listen to what you have to say."

The Hardys decided to meet with the writer on familiar ground. They took their van, and Richards followed them in his car to Mr. Pizza, one of their favorite hangouts at the mall. Their friend Tony Prito worked part-time at the restaurant, and he gave the Hardys and Richards a quiet booth in the back.

"The timing is perfect," Richards said eagerly after they ordered. "If I write a book about you now, it's practically guaranteed to sell hundreds of thousands of copies."

"Why is that?" Frank responded.

Richards lowered his voice to a confidential tone. "My latest book hasn't come out yet, but the publishing industry is buzzing about it. It's going to be a mega-hit."

He sat back, his eyes unfocused as he stared off into the distance. "Before you know it, I'll be flying all over the country for talk shows and book signings. My name will be a household word."

"We still don't know anything specific about the action-adventure thrillers you tell us you write," Frank pointed out.

Richards took an adventure magazine out of

the backpack he used as a briefcase and placed it on the table.

"What's this?" Joe asked, picking up the magazine.

"The first chapter of my new book is printed in there," Richards said. "I did a lot of research on federal undercover operations and came up with this story line about an ultrasecret government security agency called the NET—the National Elite Task force. The agency is run by a mysterious superagent, whose name nobody knows. They just call him Mr. Green."

This comment drew Frank's full attention. The similarity to the very real—and top secret—Network and its top operative, the Gray Man, was more than a little spooky. The Hardys had worked with the Gray Man and the Network more than once, and Frank wasn't eager to get mixed up with the agency again.

"So," he said, forcing himself to sound casual, "what's the plot of your book?"

Richards's eyes lit up. "It's a great story. You see, this international terrorist group hijacks a shipment of weapons-grade plutonium from a U.S. military installation, and—"

Two large, dark shadows suddenly fell across the booth. Frank raised his head and peered into the stern faces of a pair of steely-eyed, broad-shouldered men dressed in expensive suits.

"Oliver Richards?" one of the men asked, his eyes fastened on the writer.

"Who wants to know?" Joe responded.

"None of your business," the other man growled. He reached out and laid a hand on the writer's arm. "Get up. You're coming with us."

"Hey, wait a minute," Joe protested, starting to get up as the man dragged Richards out of the booth.

"Don't move," the first man commanded in an ice-cold voice. He pulled his suit jacket back, far enough to reveal the butt of an automatic pistol in a shoulder holster.

Frank's gaze darted from the gun to his brother, who was already halfway out of his seat. Frank only had a split second to choose between following Joe's lead or stopping him. He knew either choice might prove fatal.

FRANK FIRMLY PUT A hand on his brother's shoulder, pushing him back down into his seat. "Everybody, take it easy," Frank urged, his eyes riveted on the man with the gun.

The man's hand rested on the butt of the automatic. "Good idea," he said flatly. "Things could get ugly if you make a scene."

"It already looks pretty ugly from where I'm standing," Richards spoke up, struggling against the grip of the man's partner. "Do you really think you can drag me out of this restaurant in front of all these witnesses?"

The man with the gun smiled thinly. "That's what we get paid to do." His hand drifted from the butt of the pistol to the inside pocket of his jacket. "We're federal agents," he said, briefly flashing a badge with a photo ID. "And we're taking you in for questioning, Mr. Richards."

Frank studied the man carefully. "Let me have a look at that badge," he challenged.

The man glared down at him, his smile twisting into a scowl. "Don't push your luck, punk." He turned to his partner with a curt nod, and they headed out of the restaurant with the writer in tow.

"You can't get away with this!" Richards protested. He cast a desperate glance at the Hardys. "*Do* something!" he pleaded.

Frank and Joe and a handful of gaping onlookers watched helplessly as the two well-built men shoved the writer into a brown sedan with a flashing blue light mounted on the dashboard.

Tony Prito came over to the table where Frank and Joe were sitting. The Hardys were staring out the window watching as the car sped away. "What was that all about?" Tony Prito asked Frank. "I was working the cash register when those two characters came in. Before I could say anything, one of them stuck a badge in my face and told me to go make a pizza and stay out of the way."

"Did you get a good look at the badge?" Frank asked.

Tony shook his head.

"Neither did I," Frank said. "They claimed they were federal agents."

"That's sort of vague, isn't it?" Joe remarked. "I mean, if they were FBI or CIA, wouldn't they say so?"

"That bothered me too," Frank responded. "I think we'd better call the police."

A Bayport police squad car showed up at the pizzeria a few minutes after Tony made the call. Frank was relieved to see the familiar face of Officer Con Riley. The Hardys could always count on Riley to listen and not dismiss their claims simply because they were teenagers.

Officer Riley jotted down a few notes as Frank, Joe, and Tony took turns telling him what had happened. "Did anybody get the license plate number of the car?" he finally asked.

"I caught a glimpse of the plate when they took off out of the mall parking lot," Frank answered. "It started with the letters GDA, followed by a three, or maybe an eight."

"Okay," Riley said. "I'll radio it in, and we'll see what we can find out. I'll let you know if anything turns up."

Frank didn't get very much sleep that night. He recalled what Richards had told them about his new book. On a few of the Hardys' cases, they had crossed paths with the Gray Man and his ultrasecret government agency, the Network.

Network agents addressed the Gray Man as "Mr. Gray," and Frank thought that was uncannily close to Richards's fictional secret agent, "Mr. Green." Frank hated coincidences, and this one was a little too close for comfort.

He got up early and spent time at his computer, using the modem to tap into international electronic bulletin boards and databases. He didn't have much luck uncovering information on the writer who had vanished as abruptly as he had appeared.

Joe wandered into Frank's room late in the morning, just as Frank was logging off the computer. "So that's what you've been doing," Joe said. "Cruising the digital freeway for information?"

Frank sighed. "It's not exactly free, and it's more like a maze of side streets without road signs."

Joe nodded. "I know what you mean. Sometimes I feel like roadkill on the information highway."

Con Riley showed up at the Hardys' house around noon and found Frank and Joe letting off steam by sparring in the backyard. Frank countered Joe's sharp boxing jabs with a slick combination of fluid karate moves.

From the police officer's grim expression, Frank knew Riley wasn't bringing good news.

"I think it would be best if you forgot you

ever met Oliver Richards," the police officer told the Hardys.

"You know we can't do that," Frank replied.

Riley sighed. "Let me put it another way. Consider this a direct police order from very high up."

"From Chief Collig?" Joe responded. Joe knew the Bayport police chief would go out of his way to keep the Hardys off a case.

"Higher than that even," Riley said. "We made some routine calls to a few federal agencies, like the FBI. We got stonewalled everywhere. Then Chief Collig got a phone call that didn't do anything to improve his usual grumpy mood.

"After the call the chief announced that the Richards case was a federal matter," Riley continued. "It's officially out of the jurisdiction of the Bayport police."

"I'll bet that made him mad," Joe said.

Riley chuckled dryly. "Not nearly as mad as the fact that a couple of teenagers named Hardy started the chain of events that brought all this federal heat down on him."

Frank frowned. "This is all just a little too far out of whack. Who called Chief Collig? What federal agency is behind this? Where is Richards now? Has he been charged with a crime?"

"I can't answer any of your questions," Riley said.

"You mean you *won't*," Frank countered.

"No," Riley responded. "I mean I can't because I don't know the answers. And if the chief knows, he's not talking. It's a 'national security' matter, and it's none of our business."

"So that's the official line?" Joe said sarcastically.

"I don't like it any more than you do," Riley said. "But there's nothing I can do." He gave the Hardys a stern look. "And you'd better not even try."

"Try what?" Joe responded. "What do you think we're going to do?"

"I don't know," the police officer muttered, "And I hope I don't find out." With those words, he turned and walked away.

Joe turned to his brother. "We have to find Richards."

"I know," Frank reluctantly agreed. "But that's *all* we're going to do. Whatever his scheme is, I don't want any part of it."

The Hardys walked to the front of the house and watched as Riley drove off in his squad car. Just then Frank saw Chet Morton lumbering into view down the block. Frank watched their large friend amble up the sidewalk with a slow, deliberate stride.

"Wasn't that Con Riley?" Chet asked when he reached the Hardys.

"Yep," Joe answered.

"What was he doing here?" Chet asked.

"It's a long story," Frank said. "What are *you* doing here?"

"Don't tell me you forgot," Chet responded. "We have a softball game in twenty minutes. Everybody's going to be there. Biff, Tony, Phil, Callie, Vanessa—"

Frank slapped his forehead. "I *did* forget!"

"So did I," Joe said. "And to tell the truth, I don't feel much like playing ball right now."

"Aw, come on," Chet said. "You have to go. I was counting on you guys to give me a ride to the park."

The Hardys took a few minutes to gather their baseball gear—bats, balls, mitts, caps—inside the house while Chet waited in the driveway. Then, as the three friends were piling into the van, a car pulled up in front of the house, and they all turned to watch as Oliver Richards got out. The writer's long brown hair was tied back in a ponytail, and Frank noted that the man hadn't shaved. Put a patch over one eye, Frank thought, and with his earring Richards could be a pirate.

"Where have you been?" Joe called out, rushing over to Richards. "What happened?"

"Boy, that was really something last night, wasn't it?" Richards responded, making it sound like a harmless adventure.

"I guess you could say that," Frank replied, a little disconcerted by Richards's cheerful tone. "Are you all right?"

"Oh, sure," the writer said. "Those two guys put on a tough act, but they were just trying to scare me."

"They did a pretty good job," Joe remarked. "You acted petrified when they grabbed you."

"I guess I was," the writer admitted with a chuckle. "And I guess I should be upset about the whole incident, but I can't help feeling a little flattered."

Joe stared at him blankly. "Huh?"

"I've never gotten this kind of attention before," Richards explained. "Apparently, my research and guesswork came fairly close to the truth this time. Somebody in the federal government read the excerpt of my new book in that magazine and got very nervous. So they sent out a couple of agents to haul me in for questioning."

"That still bothers me," Frank said. "What kind of agents were they? What government agency sent them?"

Richards's expression was puzzled. "You know, that's funny. I never did find out. They took me to some office building and grilled me about my sources. They must have asked me the same questions a hundred times."

"What did you tell them?" Frank asked. "Where *did* you get the information for your book?"

"A good writer never reveals his sources," Richards replied in a mock serious tone. "Besides," he added, "what makes you think I'd tell you something that a couple of trained professionals couldn't drag out of me?"

"I hate to interrupt," Chet interjected, "but we should get going. Everybody's waiting for us at the ballpark."

"Sounds like fun," Richards said. "I love baseball."

"You wouldn't like this," Frank said, trying to discourage the writer. "Our games are really boring—and we don't have room for any more players."

Richards smiled. "That's okay. I'll just watch. And take notes," he added, pulling a notebook from his pocket.

Richards followed them to the park and watched the softball game from the bleachers on one side of the baseball diamond. It was a grudge match. A week earlier Frank, Callie, Chet, and Tony Prito had pounded Joe's team.

Joe hoped Biff Hooper would deliver at the plate this time. Phil Cohen and Vanessa were pretty good players, but Biff was the home-run king. Almost as large as Chet and all muscle, Biff could pulverize the ball—if only he could connect.

Joe groaned as Biff struck out for the third time in a row in the bottom of the third inning, another victim of Callie's deadly sinker.

Joe picked up his mitt and headed out onto

the field. As he was limbering up for a few practice throws before the beginning of the fourth inning, he noticed a black sedan pull up to the curb at the edge of the park. Joe froze in his tracks and his eyes bulged as two men in military fatigues burst out of the car. Both men wore ski masks and carried Calico M-950 automatic pistols.

"Hey!" Richards cried out as the two masked men raced up into the bleachers. "What's going on?" The only answer he got was a sharp jab in the stomach with the barrel of a gun. Richards grunted and doubled over. The two men roughly grabbed him and dragged him out of the bleachers.

"Stop!" Joe called out, taking off after them with Frank right behind.

One of the masked men whirled around and aimed his weapon at the Hardys. Fire spat out of the short barrel. Joe dove to one side and Frank rolled the other way. The ground in front of them erupted as a stream of bullets slammed into the dirt.

By the time the Hardys got up, the kidnappers had forced Richards into the black sedan. The Hardys rushed out into the street as the car sped away. A horn blasted behind them, and they jumped back to the curb. A taxi screeched past, and the two brothers caught a glimpse of the man in the backseat.

Frank and Joe stared as the two cars disappeared around the corner with tires squealing.

"Did you see the guy in the back of that cab?" Joe asked his brother.

Frank nodded.

"It was him, wasn't it?" Joe said.

"That's right," Frank said grimly. "It was the Gray Man."

Chapter

4

THE HARDYS WENT straight to police headquarters, and this time they had a half-dozen witnesses. Callie, Vanessa, and the rest of the gang were all there to back them up.

"They can't just sweep it under the rug this time," Joe muttered as a uniformed sergeant led them into Chief Collig's office.

The chief listened in stony silence as the Hardys described the masked gunmen who had kidnapped Oliver Richards. Although their friends hadn't been as close to the action as the Hardys, they had seen enough to back up the story. Nobody else had seen the Gray Man, and the Hardys decided to leave out that one detail for now.

"This is a very serious situation," the chief said

stiffly. He looked over at the sergeant. "Take these kids to the conference room and write up their statements." His sharp gaze shifted to Frank and Joe. "You two stay here. I want to ask you a few questions."

Chief Collig shuffled some papers on his desktop as the others filed out of the office. Then he glared across the desk at Frank and Joe. "I told Con Riley to deliver a message to you this morning. Didn't you get it?"

"We got it," Joe answered.

"Maybe Riley didn't make it clear enough," the police chief said. "Let me clarify the situation,"

"The message was quite clear," Frank said, "but the situation has changed now, don't you think?"

"No!" Chief Collig snapped, red-faced. "It hasn't!" He stopped and took a deep breath. "What I'm about to tell you goes no further than this room. Do you understand?"

Frank and Joe nodded in unison.

"Oliver Richards is involved with a very dangerous terrorist group."

"Do you have proof of that?" Frank asked. He didn't trust Richards absolutely, but he didn't think he was a terrorist, either.

"I can't tell you any of the details," Collig responded, "but Richards has been under federal surveillance ever since he got to Bayport. I don't know what really happened at the park," he continued, "and neither do you. But I can assure you that federal agents are on top of it."

"If you don't know what happened," Joe countered, "you don't know who's on top of what."

The police chief cut him off. "You're way out of line, young man."

"Those guys shot at us!" Joe exclaimed. "And you're just going to let them walk away?"

"We don't know *who* shot at you," the police chief retorted. "It might have been terrorist buddies of Richards. And I'm not going to interfere with a critical federal undercover operation to find out."

"I can't believe this," Joe grumbled.

Chief Collig heaved a sigh. "Do you think I like this, Joe? My hands are tied. This case is officially closed for me—and for you, too."

"What do we do now?" Joe asked his brother when they got home. "The Gray Man has a lot of clout. If he doesn't want us to find out what's going on, we won't."

"But this whole operation is too heavy-handed for the Network," Frank noted.

"Yeah," Joe agreed. "And I find it hard to believe that Richards is a terrorist."

"So do I," Frank stated, his forehead furrowed. "Well, if the police can't do anything, we'll just have to go right to the source."

Joe looked at his brother. "What did you have in mind?"

"We have the unlisted phone number for the Gray Man's office in Washington. Let's give him a call."

"Do you think he'll tell us anything?"

Frank shrugged. "There's only one way to find out."

Using the phone next to the computer in his room, Frank dialed the unlisted number.

"Grayco Enterprises," a woman's brusque voice answered after two rings.

"Yes," Frank spoke into the phone. "Could I speak to Mr. Gray, please?"

There was a pause on the other end of the line. "Ah, Mr. Gray isn't available right now," the woman finally responded. Frank detected an edge of tension in her voice. "Would you like to leave a message?"

"Never mind," Frank said. "Maybe I'll try again later."

"If you could just give me your name—" the woman said hastily. "I can assure you he'll call back as soon as possible."

"It's really not important," Frank responded.

"How did you get this number?" the woman pressed.

Frank hung up the phone.

"Why did you do that?" Joe asked.

"Something's wrong," Frank said. "The woman

who answered the phone acted as if a call for Mr. Gray was the last thing in the world she expected."

"Maybe he doesn't get a lot of phone calls at the office," Joe suggested.

Frank shook his head. "I have a bad feeling about this."

Late the next morning Joe noticed a drab gray panel truck pull up and park across the street from the Hardys' house. When it was still there half an hour later, Joe called his brother over to the window.

"I thought it might be a delivery truck," Joe said. "But it's just sitting there. Nobody has gotten in or out."

"There aren't markings of any kind on it," Frank observed. "A delivery or repair truck would at least have a company name."

Joe's eyes widened. "Do you think it's the Net—" He cut himself off and silently motioned for Frank to follow him into the bathroom.

Joe closed the door and turned on the water in both the sink and bathtub. "Okay," he said in a whisper barely louder than the rushing water. "I think it's safe to talk now."

"What made you think it wasn't safe before?" Frank responded.

"If the Gray Man sent a Network team to keep

an eye on us," Joe explained, "that truck could be bristling with electronic eavesdropping gear."

"If that's a Network surveillance truck," Frank said, "then we can't just hang around here and chat."

"Any ideas?" Joe responded. "The van's parked in the driveway out front. If they see us drive off, they'll just follow."

"I know," Frank said. "That's why we're going to slip out the back way."

"We can't get very far on foot," Joe pointed out.

"With any luck, we won't have to," Frank said.

The Hardys slipped out the back door, darted across the neighbors' backyard, and came out on a side street. Then they headed for the nearest gas station, where Frank made a quick call from a pay phone. A few minutes later Callie Shaw drove into the gas station, and the Hardys jumped into her car.

Frank filled Callie in, then told her to drive to the police station. "Why?" Callie asked. "Chief Collig wouldn't help before. Why do you think he'd change his mind now?"

"He won't," Frank said. "The chief plays by the book." He glanced at his watch as Callie pulled up in front of the police station. "Con Riley gets off duty in a few minutes. If anybody knows what's going on around here, he will."

Frank got out of Callie's car when he saw Con

Riley coming out of the building. Riley scowled as Frank walked up to him. "If this is about the Richards case," Riley said, "forget it."

Frank followed the police officer down the sidewalk, away from the police station. "Come on, Con," Frank pleaded. "Richards was snatched right in front of us, and the guys who did it tried to ventilate Joe and me. I think we deserve a better explanation than the official bunk we got from the chief."

Riley glanced around to make sure no one was nearby. "Okay," he practically whispered. "But we can't talk here. Meet me at the park in half an hour."

Callie waited in the car while Frank and Joe met Con Riley at the park near the spot where Richards had been abducted.

"I'm only doing this to satisfy your curiosity so you'll stay out of trouble," Riley said.

"Thanks, Con," Joe said. "We owe you one."

Riley snorted. "I'll put it on your tab."

"So what's the real story?" Frank pressed.

"I don't know all the details," Riley replied. "But there was a major foul-up with some federal undercover job. Just before my shift ended today, we got a notice to arrest a federal operative who had turned double agent."

"Double agent?" Frank echoed. "You mean

37

he's selling our government secrets to some foreign country?"

"I don't know," Riley replied. "But it must be something like that. Word is, the official charge is treason."

"The guy is a traitor?" Joe reacted. "Who is this agent?"

Riley pulled a folded sheet of paper out of his coat pocket. "The guy has a list of aliases a mile long. But we got this fax of a recent picture of him."

The police officer unfolded a glossy sheet of paper and showed it to the Hardys. Frank and Joe stared at the bland, unremarkable face.

It was a face they could never forget—the face of the Gray Man.

Chapter

5

FRANK AND JOE GAPED at the grainy fax copy of the photograph. There was no doubt in Frank's mind. It was definitely the Gray Man, one of the top members of the Network. Now Con Riley was claiming he was a double agent!

"What's the matter?" Riley asked, breaking the awkward silence. "You act like you saw a ghost. Do you know this guy?"

"Um, no," Frank responded. "I was just thinking how normal this guy looks."

"Uh, yeah," Joe quickly added, "like an accountant or a banker or something." Very few people knew about the Hardys' work with the Gray Man, and Con Riley wasn't one of them.

The police officer eyed the two brothers suspiciously. "What's going on here?"

"*You're* supposed to tell *us* that," Frank said. "What do you know about this double agent? If he's not on our side, who's he working for?"

"That's the part I don't get," Joe said. "Who are the bad guys?"

Riley snatched back the creased sheet of paper. "You two never give up, do you? I've told you everything I know." He leveled his best, stern cop gaze at the Hardys and shifted to a lecturing tone. "This isn't a kid's game. Stay clear of this case. This man is considered armed and dangerous."

"Ah-hah!" Joe retorted. "*That's* something you didn't tell us."

Riley rolled his eyes. "Okay, now you know everything." He folded up the paper and stuck it back in his pocket. "Don't make me sorry I talked to you. And whatever you do, don't go looking for this character on your own."

As soon as Frank and Joe got in the car, Callie wanted to know what Con had told them.

"The police are looking for the Gray Man," Frank told her. "If they find him, they'll arrest him."

"The Gray Man?" Callie responded. "Why do the police want to arrest him? What are the charges?"

"That part's a little fuzzy," Joe said. "Riley

said the Gray Man is a double agent. But who would he be working for?"

"Those thugs who grabbed Richards didn't act like Network agents," Frank noted.

"You're right," Joe replied. "Network agents have stuck guns in our faces before, but they'd never blast away at unarmed bystanders."

"Who would?" Callie asked.

Frank was silent for a moment, then turned and focused on his brother.

Joe knew what his brother was thinking. "The Assassins," he said grimly. He wished he could forget he had ever heard the name of that terrorist group. In the boys' first clash with the vicious band—a bitter struggle that had claimed the life of Iola Morton, Joe's girlfriend and Chet Morton's sister—they had come out the losers.

Frank nodded. "Every time we cross paths with the Gray Man, the Assassins are involved somehow."

"Chief Collig said Richards was involved with a terrorist group," Joe recalled. "Terrorism is the Assassins' stock-in-trade. They'll hire themselves out as killers to anyone who can pay the price."

Callie frowned and shook her head. "I thought the Gray Man was dedicated to wiping out the Assassins. Why would he suddenly switch sides and help them? And why would the Gray Man have any interest in Richards?"

"The main character in Richards's new book

is a dead ringer for the Gray Man," Frank said. "He might be worried about how much Richards really knows—and what he could reveal."

"Okay," Callie said. "That makes sense. But what about the Assassins? What's their connection? And why would the Gray Man flip to their side?"

"That's the question," Frank said. "We need more information before we can even begin to answer it."

"We don't have proof that the Assassins are involved," Joe added in a hollow voice. But deep down he knew they had to be involved, and he also knew he and Frank would have to deal with the deadly international terrorists before getting to the bottom of this case. He desperately hoped they could avoid paying the terrible price they'd paid when Iola was killed.

Frank peered out the window as Callie neared their house. "Don't stop," he cautioned. "Drive by slowly."

"I don't see any sign of that truck," Joe said.

"Neither do I," Frank said. "It looks like the coast is clear."

"Does that mean you want me to stop?" Callie asked.

"You might as well," Frank responded. "We have to go home sometime. I need access to my computer to do a little electronic digging."

Callie braked to a stop and dropped Frank and

Joe off in front of their house. "Give me a call if you find out anything," Callie said as Frank got out of the car.

"I will," Frank promised, and gave her a quick kiss.

"Thanks for helping us," Joe called back as he approached the front door with Frank. "If you're planning to hook up to any outside databases, you'll have to use the phone modem. By now, the Network could have the phone lines tapped."

Frank paused and looked at his brother. "I hadn't thought of—"

A blur of movement caught his eye. Two men burst out of a brown sedan parked halfway down the block and bolted toward the Hardys. Frank sucked in his breath. "I think we weren't big enough fish for a whole van load of Network equipment. We have new tails. Move it."

Joe turned and saw two well-built men in suits sprinting toward them. He recognized them instantly. "It's those two heavies who hauled Richards out of the restaurant!"

"Now it looks like they want to haul us somewhere," Frank responded. "And I don't think we want to go." He spun around and spotted Callie's car near the end of the block, just about to turn the corner. "Callie, wait!" he shouted, sprinting into the street, waving his arms frantically.

Frank ran up the street with Joe right behind him. Frank heard the tires screech as Callie hit the brakes and slammed her car into reverse. He glanced back over his shoulder. The two hulking men seemed even larger than he remembered from their first encounter.

Callie's tires squealed again when the car shuddered to a stop, and Frank grabbed the back door handle. He jerked the door open and threw himself inside. Joe landed on top of him a split second later.

"Take off!" Joe yelled, twisting around to yank the door shut.

"I am!" Callie shouted, throwing the Hardys off balance as she stomped on the gas pedal.

"Who were those guys?" Callie asked tensely, her hands clamped to the steering wheel, her eyes riveted on the road ahead. "Assassins?"

"I doubt it," Frank replied, climbing from the back into the front seat. "They're probably Network agents."

Callie glanced over at him. "Network agents? From the way you were hollering and running down the street, I thought somebody was trying to kill you."

"Turn right here," Frank said, pointing out the window. "I don't know what those guys had in mind. If the Gray Man really is some kind of double agent, other Network agents could be involved, too."

"Involved in what?" Callie responded.

"I wish I knew," Frank muttered. "But what-

44

ever it is, if the Gray Man is calling the shots, it's very big."

Joe groaned. "How can we tell the good guys from the bad guys? And what about Richards? Which side is he on?"

"I don't think he's on either side," Frank replied. "I think he's caught in the middle—like us."

"So what do we do now?" Callie asked.

"For now," Frank answered, "we steer clear of everybody."

Callie glanced in the rearview mirror. "That might be a little tricky. Look behind us."

Joe turned his head and peered out the rear window. The brown sedan was turning the corner behind them. He could see two men inside. "That's them, all right."

"Maybe we can lose them," Callie said, nudging the gas pedal and edging over the speed limit.

"You'll have to do better than that," Joe said, watching the car behind them. "They're gaining on us."

"Hang a left at the next intersection," Frank told Callie.

Joe turned around to study the road ahead. "No, turn right!"

"Left or right?" Callie snapped. "Make up your minds!"

"Right!" Joe repeated forcefully as the car nosed into the intersection.

45

Callie turned the steering wheel hard. The tires screeched in protest, and the back end of the car fishtailed wildly, tossing Joe around in the backseat.

A horn blared, and an oncoming truck swerved around Callie's car on the right.

"We're going the wrong way!" Frank exclaimed. "This is a one-way street!"

Callie dodged another car speeding toward them.

"Look out!" Frank shouted. "We must have a red light!"

"What light?" Callie reacted hotly, stomping on the brakes. "We're going the wrong way on a one-way street. We can't *have* a light!"

The car skidded to a halt in the middle of the intersection. Cars coming at them from both sides screeched to a stop. Horns blasted, and drivers yelled out their windows.

"I think I'll turn left here," Callie said in a slow, even voice barely containing her rage. "Don't you guys think that'd be a good idea? At least we'll be driving in the right direction."

Joe was about to reply, but a sharp glance from his brother silenced him.

"Look on the bright side," Joe ventured after Callie had turned. "It looks as if we lost the guys who were chasing us."

"On the down side," Frank responded, "we can't risk going back to our house."

"Where do you want to go?" Callie asked. "We can't drive around all day."

Joe's stomach whispered to him in a low grumble. "I'm hungry. Let's go grab a pizza."

Tony Prito was on duty that afternoon at Mr. Pizza. He was full of questions as he served the Hardys and Callie a large pepperoni pizza, but the restaurant was too busy for him to hang around to hear the answers.

"The way I see it," Frank told Joe and Callie, after taking a big bite of his third slice, "there are two possibilities. The first is that the guys who chased us are renegade agents, possibly working with the Gray Man on some illegal scheme. Although I have a hard time buying the idea that the Gray Man has turned."

"And the second option?" Callie asked, getting Frank back on track.

"The Network put a tail on us," Frank replied, "hoping we'll lead them to the Gray Man."

Joe frowned. "Neither one explains why those apes were so determined to catch us."

"The first one doesn't," Frank admitted. "But remember, we had already evaded Network surveillance once."

Joe grasped his brother's logic. "So if they were legitimate agents on the trail of a traitor, they might try a more direct approach the second time."

47

"Hold on," Callie said in a hesitant tone. "Why would the Network put a tail on you?"

Joe chuckled. "They probably have a file on us thicker than an unabridged dictionary. We've run into Mr. Gray more than once."

"And we called his office from our house," Frank added. "The Network has electronic gear that most people never even dreamed of. They probably knew who was calling before the receptionist picked up the phone."

Callie reached for the bill that Tony Prito had left on the table. "What's my share?" she asked.

"That's okay, we'll pick up the tab," Frank said.

Joe checked his wallet and gave his brother a sheepish look. "Um, I seem to be a little low on cash right now."

Frank gave him a practiced scowl. "How much do you have?"

Joe pulled a single, crumpled dollar bill out of his wallet.

Frank sighed and rolled his eyes. "I should start charging you interest," he muttered.

Frank got up and walked over to the cash register. He handed the money to Tony, who just pushed it back at him.

"It's been covered," Tony said.

Frank gave him a puzzled look. "What do you mean?"

48

Tony pointed to a dark booth in the corner. "The guy over there paid for your pizza."

Frank turned—and tried not to gawk. A slight smile drifted across the bland face of the man sitting in the booth. The face was utterly unremarkable, yet completely unmistakable.

Frank was staring at the Gray Man.

Chapter

6

FRANK APPROACHED the secluded booth at the back of the restaurant. "You've been showing up in some strange places lately," he said, sliding into the seat across the table from the Gray Man.

Joe and Callie quickly joined them.

"The last couple of days have been full of surprises," the Gray Man said.

"You've got that right," Joe said coolly. "And most of them seem to lead right to you."

Frank studied the harmless-looking man carefully. He appeared to be calm and relaxed, but Frank could read signs of stress in his eyes. "We saw you at the park when Richards was kidnapped," Frank told him.

"I saw you, too," the Gray Man replied. "That

50

was a pretty foolish thing you did—chasing after those men. They could have cut you in half with their assault weapons."

"And who would have been responsible for that?" Joe growled. "Did they have orders to kill anybody who got in their way?"

"They don't need orders to shoot to kill," the Gray Man said. "For them, it's the simplest way out of most encounters. That's just the way they work."

"And who were they working for?" Frank prodded, watching the Gray Man's eyes.

"Not for me," the Gray Man said evenly, returning Frank's steady gaze. "I know the situation appears to be bad, but I was following Richards," he explained. "Waiting for a chance to talk to him alone."

"You mean you didn't want any witnesses," Joe countered.

The Gray Man turned his gaze to Joe. "Think about it for a minute. If I wanted Richards to disappear, I could make it happen in a blink. And it wouldn't be in broad daylight in front of a dozen eyewitnesses."

Frank could see the cold logic of what the Gray Man implied, and it made him shudder. As one of the top people in the Network, the Gray Man wielded immense—and deadly—power. If he decided someone should vanish off the face of the earth, the victim's own family wouldn't be able to find him. The trail would be instantly cold, if not completely erased.

"I'm lost," Callie spoke up. "What's so important about this writer? You wanted to talk to him. A pair of federal agents grilled him, and then he got abducted at gunpoint. What is it about this guy?"

"Oliver Richards's new book contains some, ah, disturbing information," the Gray Man replied, eyeing Callie uncomfortably. "A few weeks ago we uncovered a plot by the Assassins to hijack a shipment of plutonium."

"What would they do with a load of radioactive material?" Callie asked.

"Build nuclear weapons," Frank said grimly.

"Or sell the plutonium to anybody else who might want to build a nuclear arsenal," the Gray Man suggested.

"That sounds a lot like the plot of Richards's new book," Joe noted.

The Gray Man nodded. "You aren't the only one who noticed that. We were closing in on the terrorists when the first chapter of Richards's book appeared in that adventure magazine. We had a group of suspected Assassins under surveillance. Suddenly they split up and vanished like smoke. When I read what was in that magazine, it seemed like too much of a coincidence, so I sent a team of agents to question Richards."

"You mean the two who dragged him out of

here yesterday?" Joe grumbled. "They followed us today. I guess they thought we knew something about Richards."

"I didn't ask them to follow you," the Gray Man said. "They must have taken it on themselves after Richards refused to tell them anything."

"So you decided to try yourself," Frank ventured.

Joe spotted Vanessa walking into the restaurant and waved her over to the booth.

The Gray Man glanced up and frowned. "Why don't you just call all your friends and invite them to join us? We'll turn this into a big party."

"We don't have to call anybody," Joe said. "If we stay here long enough, our whole gang will show up. This is one of our favorite hangouts."

The Gray Man sighed. "I know. That's why I came here looking for you."

Vanessa wedged into the booth next to Joe. Then he turned back to the Gray Man. "Why were you looking for us?"

The Gray Man shifted in his seat and cleared his throat. "Can we talk in private?" he said. "Would you ladies please excuse us?" he continued, addressing Vanessa and Callie. "The information I'm about to reveal is highly confidential and could be dangerous to anyone in possession of it. I don't want to put you at risk."

With that he stood and suggested that Joe and Frank join him outside the mall. Once the three had found a quiet, out-of-the-way corner in the parking lot, they continued their conversation. "I need your help," he said.

"So," Joe said, "you want *our* help? What about the Network helping you?"

"I'm not with the Network just now," the Gray Man responded. "After Richards's article came out I was suspended while they investigated—"

"But—" Joe started to interrupt.

"Yes, yes, I know—I told you that I had ordered my men to question Richards after the magazine appeared, but I was working without agency approval. Then after Richards was snatched, the agency decided that I had kidnapped him to shut him up about any of my secret dealings. At that point I went into hiding because I was being hunted by the agency."

"Wait a minute. You're pretty high up in the Network. Who can order you around?" Joe asked, confused.

The Gray Man gave a low chuckle. "In an agency such as the Network there is always one more layer of authority."

"But there must have been some evidence for them to go after you," Frank continued, probing.

The Gray Man chuckled again, more bitterly this time. "In a position like mine, the slightest hint of wrongdoing is enough for them to assume you're guilty. I am now in the position of having to prove my innocence."

"That's totally against the principles of our

legal system," Joe said. "You're supposed to be innocent till proven guilty."

"Sometimes the Network takes a loose approach to the letter of the law," the Gray Man said bluntly. He tapped the side of his head with his index finger. "There's enough classified information up here to blow our national defense system wide open."

"But why did they tell the police you're a double agent and wanted for treason?" Joe asked.

"What would you say if you wanted the police to work overtime to help you capture someone?"

Joe took all this in and finally spoke. "So what do you want us to do?" he asked a little curtly. "Go tell your invisible bosses what a swell guy you are so you can get your job back?" In all the Hardys' dealings with the Gray Man, Joe had never completely trusted him.

"My only concern right now is for Richards's safety," the Gray Man contended.

"Do you think the Assassins have him?" Frank asked.

The Gray Man nodded.

"Do you think Richards's book is too close to the truth to be a freak coincidence?" Frank asked.

"It seems it was close enough for them to kidnap Richards to find out how much more he knows and where he got his information," the Gray Man replied. "And once they find that out ..." His voice trailed off, and Frank picked up his thought.

"That's when they'll decide they don't need him anymore, and they'll kill him without a second thought."

"Can't the Network help him?" Joe asked.

"They think they are," the Gray Man answered. "They've decided I took him. So every available agent is out combing this city for me— which is why I need your help," he continued. "I can't do this alone."

Frank glanced at Joe, and Joe was slow to nod his approval. "Count us in," Frank finally said. "We'll meet you in the park in forty-five minutes."

"We can't do much while we're hanging around the mall," Joe remarked. "We'll need wheels to get around. But with agents watching the house, there's no way we can get the van without being tailed."

"Oh, I think we can figure out a way," Frank said confidently.

The Hardys went into their house through the back door, to avoid confronting the men out front. Frank turned and held a finger to his lips to warn Callie and Vanessa not to speak. The girls had been recruited to help out. If the Network had electronic surveillance gear trained on the house, the only voices they'd hear would be Frank's and Joe's.

"Hey, Joe," Frank spoke in a loud, clear voice. "Let's take a ride over to the mall."

"Sounds good to me," Joe boomed cheerfully. "Let me grab a jacket." He opened the front hall closet and pulled out two baseball jackets and passed them over to Callie and Vanessa. It was a little warm out for jackets, but the girls would need the extra padding to pull off their plan.

Joe rummaged around the top shelf of the closet and found two baseball caps. Callie and Vanessa put on the caps, stuffing their hair into them. Vanessa slipped on a pair of aviator sunglasses and grinned. "How do I look?" she mouthed, doing a slow, full turn.

Like the Hardys, the girls were both wearing jeans and sneakers. With a little luck, Joe told himself, they might just be able to pull this one off.

Callie buttoned up Frank's jacket and put on the sunglasses that Frank handed her.

Frank handed Callie the keys to the van. "Don't overdo it," he wrote on a pad of paper he had picked up in the living room. "Just get in the van and drive straight to the mall."

If everything went according to plan, the Network agents would tail the van to the mall. But when Callie and Vanessa got out of the van, they wouldn't be wearing their disguises anymore.

When the agents realized they'd been tricked, they'd head back to the house, looking for the Hardys. Frank and Joe would be long gone by then, heading for the mall in Callie's car, which had been parked one street over.

The Hardys peeked out the window as Callie and Vanessa strolled out the front door and got in the van. When the van rolled down the street, the familiar brown sedan pulled away from the curb and followed.

"So far, so good," Joe whispered when both vehicles were out of sight. "Now it's time for stage two."

The Hardys padded through the house and silently slipped out the back door. Frank made sure the door was locked while Joe kept watch on the yard.

All was quiet, but within seconds Joe heard a rustling in the bushes that separated the Hardys' yard from their neighbor's.

"Hey, Frank, we're not alone anymore!" Joe yelled as the rustling changed to a crashing and the bushes parted to reveal two black-clad figures. The crouching silhouettes rose and charged Frank and Joe, the black barrels of their deadly assault weapons locked on the brothers, who were trapped on the tiny back porch.

Chapter

7

WHEN FRANK TURNED to confront the scowling man who had trained a Calico Model 900 on him in a two-fisted grip, he knew this was not a Network agent. The man had a thick mustache and a shadow of coarse beard growth. The other man had unruly, black hair, badly in need of a trim. In contrast, Network agents were uniformly clean-cut.

Joe's thoughts were running along the same track. "If this is about that overdue book from the library," he said, "I can explain."

The two black-clad terrorists stared up at him. "I had no idea the library police were so serious about unpaid fines," Joe rattled on.

"Shut up, smart aleck," the black-haired man barked harshly. "You're coming with us."

"Wait," Frank said quickly, his mind racing. "The book's right inside, let me get it for you."

He turned toward the door—then whirled back around, swinging his right leg out in a sweeping roundhouse karate kick. The mustached terrorist tried to dodge the blow and collided with his companion. Joe leapt forward off the porch and gave the man with the unruly hair a hard shove, knocking him off his feet.

The man with the mustache whipped the barrel of his gun toward Joe, but Frank lashed out with another karate kick, slamming the heel of his shoe into the side of the autoloader. Blue fire spat out the barrel. The weapon chattered and punched a wavy, dotted line of ragged holes across the back of the Hardys' house, sending wood splinters flying.

"Run for it!" Frank yelled.

Joe bolted across the yard, hard on his brother's heels. "If these guys don't kill us, Mom and Dad will when they find out somebody drilled a dozen peepholes in the back wall!"

Frank slipped through the same bushes the terrorists had emerged from and dashed across the adjoining yard to Callie's car. He threw open the passenger door and dove inside, scrambling into the driver's seat and slamming the key into the ignition.

Joe dove in right behind him. "Get us out of here!" he shouted.

Frank twisted the key and pumped the gas pedal. The engine coughed and sputtered. He felt as though he'd run a four-minute mile in the few seconds it took for the engine to catch. Frank hit the gas hard, and the car peeled away from the curb.

Joe whipped his head around and saw the man with the mustache rush into the middle of the street behind them. "Duck!" he blurted out as the man opened fire. Joe grabbed his brother's head, forcing Frank down.

"Hey!" Frank exclaimed. The car swerved wildly as the rear window exploded in a shower of glass pellets. Frank wrestled with the steering wheel and lifted his head just high enough to peer over the dashboard. He was fairly sure they were out of range now, but to be on the safe side he hunched down low behind the wheel for a few blocks.

The rest of the drive to the mall was uneventful, but Frank grimaced every time he glanced in the rearview mirror and saw the blasted remains of the back window. "Callie isn't going to be happy about this."

"It's not so bad," Joe responded. "Windows are completely covered by insurance."

Joe could tell nothing was going to brighten Frank's mood, so he changed the subject. "I didn't get a chance to check out their club membership cards, but I think it's safe to assume that our friendly visitors were Assassins."

Frank nodded. "The Assassins know we've worked with the Gray Man before, and if Richards gave them our names while being interrogated ..."

"The Assassins might think that we're all working together," Joe concluded.

"Then they'd come for us to keep us quiet," Frank added.

"Terrific," Joe muttered grimly. "Both the Assassins *and* the Network are hunting us. Now, if we could just get the FBI, the CIA, Interpol, and maybe the UN Security Council involved, we could start a cozy little softball league."

The switch in the mall parking lot went smoothly—except for when Callie found out that her car had been ventilated. Joe suggested that Callie tell her parents she came out of the mall and found the car that way, which wasn't too far from the truth. Before either Callie or Vanessa could point out how crazy it was for the Hardys to take on both the Network and the Assassins, Frank and Joe had jumped in their van and taken off.

A short drive took them to a sprawling park in the middle of town, a lush expanse of flowers and trees surrounded by an imposing gray wall of high-rise office buildings.

"We're right on schedule," Frank noted, glancing at his watch as they walked along a winding path through the exotic plants and trees in full summer bloom.

The Gray Man, with a newly acquired mustache and glasses, sat on a bench on the edge of a small pond, casually tossing bread crumbs to a growing gaggle of hungry geese. Frank and Joe sat down next to him, just in time for their meeting.

"Any problems?" the Gray Man asked.

Frank told him about their run-in with the terrorists.

"I should have known something like this would happen," the Gray Man said in a tone of dour self-reproach. "I can't ask you boys to risk your lives to help me."

"It's a little late to start worrying about that," Joe remarked.

"You can't blame yourself for this one, anyway," Frank said. "The Assassins came after us because of our connection to Richards, not to you."

"And how far could you get without us?" Joe added.

"Almost nowhere in this town," the Gray Man admitted, "I have allies who would help in other cities, but I have no contacts in Bayport other than you. And my only lead is what is now an abandoned Assassin hideout."

"Something tells me it's not conveniently located in Bayport," Joe responded.

The Gray Man shook his head. "It's just outside Denver," he revealed. "A few hundred yards from the perimeter of the Rocky Mountain Arsenal."

The name was familiar to Frank. "That's one of the places where they used to make nuclear weapons."

The Gray Man nodded. "Now the plant is being used to dismantle those same warheads. The radioactive plutonium and tritium are removed, sealed in shielded containers, and shipped to an underground storage facility. We found out the Assassins had planned to hijack one of those shipments and were watching them until we could catch them with the goods," he explained.

"When the article came out, I was suspended and the Assassins abandoned their hideout, so the whole operation unraveled too fast for the Network to sweep the house. There's a chance there are some clues in the house that could help us find the Assassins—and Richards."

"And you want us to fly to Denver to check it out," Joe ventured.

The Gray Man nodded. "The Network is looking for me, but there's no reason for them to have launched a manhunt for you. Those two men assigned to watch your house are probably the only Network agents. With a little luck, you can fly to Denver today and be back home before this time tomorrow."

The flight to Denver took four hours, but since the Hardys were flying west, when they arrived the time was only two hours later than it was in Bayport. Still, there was a limit to how long they could stretch their day. The sun was starting to sink behind the Rocky Mountains by the time they pulled away from Stapleton Airport in a rented car.

A short drive north brought them to a road that ran alongside a high chain-link fence topped with barbed wire and adorned with a combination of No Trespassing signs and stark radiation warning symbols. Joe peered through the fence and glimpsed a cluster of low buildings in the distance, beyond the scarred pit of a dried-up pond.

Frank turned left on a street lined with modest ranch houses. An older house with an overgrown lawn stood alone at the end of the street. Frank checked the address and confirmed it was the one the Assassins had used before pulling into the driveway.

"Did you bring your lock-pick set?" Joe asked as they walked up to the front door.

"Of course," Frank replied. He tested the doorknob. It turned easily, and the door swung open.

"Boy, that was amazing," Joe kidded his brother. "I didn't know you could pick a lock so fast—and without even taking out your tools."

Frank grinned. "It's all in the wrist."

Joe followed his brother inside. "I guess they didn't have much time to decorate," he observed. The only furniture in the living room was a folding card table and a matching pair of metal folding chairs.

Frank glanced around the bare room, then headed for the kitchen while Joe checked out the bedrooms.

The kitchen was as bare as the living room. Frank saw nothing in the sink or on the counters. A telephone hung on the wall next to the refrigerator. Frank was just finishing his check of the cabinets when Joe appeared in the doorway.

"Find anything?" Joe asked.

"A can of tuna and a jar of peanut butter," Frank said.

"Yum," Joe responded, smacking his lips. "Tuna and peanut butter. My favorite combination. When do we eat?"

Frank shifted from the cabinets to the drawers. "There's nothing here," he finally concluded. "Did you check the other rooms?"

"Two empty bedrooms and nothing in the bathroom," Joe informed him. "The only thing the Assassins didn't take with them was the dust."

Joe had lost hope of finding any clues as he walked over to the wall phone and lifted the receiver. "Hey, this thing is still connected," he said, holding the phone out for Frank to hear the dial tone. "Maybe we can order a pizza."

As he stood there, Joe noticed something on the floor behind the refrigerator. He hung up the phone, then crouched down and maneuvered his arm into the narrow gap between the refrigerator and the wall. He fished out a crumpled scrap of paper and smoothed it out on the side of the refrigerator.

"Check this out, Frank. Somebody must have meant this to go out with the trash," he said. "It's got a phone number written on it."

Frank walked over and scanned the numbers scrawled on the paper. Then he looked at his brother. "That's a New York City area code."

"Yep," Joe said, picking up the receiver and punching in the number. "Let's find out who our friends called."

"Able Car Rental," a woman's voice chirped. "We'd be delighted to help you with your travel needs."

"How nice," Joe responded. "The first thing I need to find out is where you are."

"Oh, we have many convenient loca—"

"I'm sure you do," Joe cut in. "And which one is this?"

"Kennedy Airport," the woman responded

cheerfully. "But we have rental offices at all the major air—"

Joe hung up the phone in the middle of her spiel and turned to his brother. "Somebody used this phone to rent a car at Kennedy Airport."

"Perfect," Frank responded. "It's a lead, anyway. We can check it out when we fly back tomorrow."

The Hardys spent the night on the floor in the deserted house and rose early the next morning for their flight back to New York. Joe was still half asleep as they left the house and climbed into their rented car. Joe stared absently at the garage door while Frank started the car.

"I just thought of something," Joe announced, abruptly getting out of the car. "We forgot to check the garage."

Frank glanced at his watch. "We don't have a lot of time."

"Come on," Joe said, walking over to the garage door. "It'll take only a couple minutes."

Frank sighed, turned off the engine, and got out of the car. He leaned against the hood and watched as Joe bent down and grabbed the handle at the bottom of the door.

"It's locked," Joe grunted, tugging on the handle.

"Forget it," Frank said. "Let's go."

"Hold on a second," Joe said, yanking hard on the handle. "I've almost got it."

Something snapped with a metallic twang, and the door creaked.

"Nothing to it!" Joe declared proudly, lifting the door with both hands.

As the door swung up and out, Joe bent down to peer under it. He realized in horror that the former tenants had left a surprise package for uninvited guests.

They had neatly taped a dozen sticks of dynamite to the back of the door. Joe froze and examined the small, black detonator attached to one end of the row of dynamite sticks. A trip wire led from the detonator to the garage door frame. By lifting the door, Joe had caused the wire to be stretched taut.

He had no idea how much more pressure it would take to snap the wire and detonate the whole "package"—and he didn't plan to stick around to find out.

Chapter

8

"GET DOWN!" JOE SHOUTED, taking off down the driveway, desperate to get away from the booby-trapped garage door.

Frank wavered, startled by Joe's sudden outburst. Joe rushed toward the car, flew into the air, sailed over the hood, and crashed down on the roof. "Move!" he bellowed, grabbing the neck of Frank's shirt and jerking him backward as he twisted and rolled over the trunk and onto the ground behind the car.

A deafening blast shattered the early morning calm. Chunks of splintered wood and jagged strips of aluminum rained down on the roof and trunk of the car. Frank and Joe cowered behind the car with their arms over their heads until the storm of flying debris subsided and the painful ringing in their ears faded.

Frank peeked around the side of the car. The garage was gone, reduced to a pile of smoldering rubble. Half the wall that the attached garage had shared with the house was blown away, too.

Joe got up and dusted himself off. "That's the worst home security system I've ever seen," he said. "A burglar could walk right into the kitchen through that hole."

"Only if his legs were still attached to his body," Frank responded.

A few people in bathrobes stumbled out of nearby houses and gaped at the wreckage.

"Let's get out of here before one of the neighbors snaps out of shock and gets our license plate number," Joe suggested.

Frank glanced at the car. A few dents seemed to be the worst of the damage. Then his gaze drifted back to the smoking remains of the garage. "I'm not even going to try to explain this to the car rental company."

It was close to one in the afternoon when the Hardys' return flight landed at Kennedy Airport. Frank and Joe followed the signs that led to the car rental area and found the Able booth.

A smiling young man in a bright red blazer greeted them. "Thank you for choosing Able," he said enthusiastically. "Do you have a reservation?"

71

"Certainly," Frank said. "Hillerman. Jerry Hillerman."

The happy clerk tapped a few keys on his computer console. "Hmm, I can't seem to find your reservation."

Frank leaned over the counter to look at the screen. "That's odd. Maybe the secretary made the reservation in the name of my associate." He gestured at Joe. "Mr. Leonard."

Joe smiled. "My friends call me Al."

The clerk tapped some more keys, and Frank watched every move. "No, I can't find anything under that name, either."

"Maybe the secretary used her own name," Joe suggested. "Try Parenski."

"No," Frank said. "She wouldn't do that." He leaned in for a closer view of the screen. "Can you search the database by phone number?"

"I think so," the clerk answered, "but I'm not really sure. I'm new here."

A line of people started to gather behind the Hardys. "Could you gentlemen step off to the side, please?" the clerk asked Frank and Joe, the cheery smile still plastered on his face. "Other customers are waiting. We have a very strict policy about timely service for our customers with reservations."

"We *have* a reservation," Frank insisted indignantly. "You just don't know how to find it. You have two computer terminals," he said, pointing

72

to the vacant terminal next to the clerk. "Can't somebody else wait on these other people?"

"It's lunchtime," the clerk explained. "I'm the only one on duty for the next half hour."

"Well, I'm not moving until we get a car," Frank announced.

"I'm sorry, sir," the clerk fretted. "All our cars are booked. Without a reservation, I can't help you. And I can't keep these other customers waiting. I could lose my job."

Frank brightened. "I've got an idea." He started to climb over the counter. "I'll give you a hand."

"You can't do that!" the clerk protested.

"Sure I can," Frank replied. His fingers started to move across the keyboard of the second terminal.

"He's a real whiz with computers," Joe assured the nervous clerk. He glanced up at the clock on the wall of the booth. "Say, that's right! Isn't this the company with the ten-minute guarantee? If you have to wait more than ten minutes, you get your car for free?"

The clerk gulped and nodded.

"Then you'd better hurry up and take care of these other folks," Joe urged.

The clerk was handing a set of car keys to the last customer in line when Frank looked up triumphantly from the computer terminal. "I found it," he declared.

The clerk sighed. "What a relief. Now if you'll just give me the reservation number, we can—"

"Forget it," Frank said, vaulting over the counter. "We've changed our minds."

"We've decided to walk," Joe told the stunned clerk.

"I did a phone number search on the car rental company's computerized database," Frank said. The Hardys and their friends were huddled in the cramped kitchen of the Mr. Pizza restaurant. "The phone number and address of the Assassins' abandoned hideout in Colorado popped up as the home information for a car rented at Kennedy Airport two days ago. According to the computer records, the car is a black, full-size, four-door sedan, license plate number BLD 128."

"Bayport's pretty big," Chet Morton said. "The eight of us can't cover all of it today. That is if they're still even in Bayport."

"Then we'll do what we can and try again in the morning," Joe responded.

"So you think the Assassins are still in town?" Phil Cohen asked.

"I have no idea," Frank admitted. "But we have to start somewhere."

"What about that government guy?" Biff Hooper asked. "What's his name? Mr. Gray? Can't he do anything?"

"He was supposed to meet us here," Frank replied. "He didn't show up, and I don't think we should wait any longer."

"Frank's right," Callie said. "I'm ready to roll."

"So am I," Vanessa joined in. "Let's do it."

Joe smiled at Vanessa.

"All right," Frank said. "We've set up a grid-search pattern. You've each got a copy of the Bayport map with your sector marked. Joe and I will coordinate the search. If you spot the car, get to the nearest phone and call us.

"And don't try to take on these guys alone," he warned. "They play for keeps."

A couple hours later the search party started to disperse because nothing had been turned up. One by one the Hardys' friends checked in and signed off for the night.

"My mom's making lasagna tonight," Chet Morton reported. "If I don't show up on time, she'll kill me."

"I've got to be at the restaurant," Tony Prito explained.

"Sure," Joe muttered after he hung up the phone. "We wouldn't want to start a pizza riot."

"I've got a flat tire," Vanessa reported. "I went to change it, but I forgot that the last time I had a flat I put on the spare and didn't have the other tire fixed."

Joe gave a deep sigh. "Where are you? We'll come get you."

The Hardys picked up Vanessa, dropped the spare off at a gas station, then drove her home. Joe offered to change the tire on her car the next day.

"I'm sorry," Vanessa said as Joe turned onto the road that led to her home on the outskirts of town. "I wanted to help, and now I feel that I'm just getting in the way."

"I'll let you know when you get in the way," Joe said.

"You were a big help," Frank added. "You covered a lot of ground before your car broke down."

"More than some other people I could name," Joe muttered.

"Nobody had any luck?" Vanessa asked.

Joe shook his head. "We're batting a perfect zero. The Assassins are probably long gone."

Frank picked up the cellular phone. "Callie hasn't checked in. I'm going to call her house." He punched in Callie's home phone number— and got a screech of electronic feedback.

"Ahhg!" he yelped, jerking the phone away from his ear.

"What's wrong?" Vanessa asked.

Frank stuck his head out the window and looked around. "It's those power lines. They scramble the phone signal every time."

A shimmer of light in a stand of trees drew Frank's gaze from the high-voltage power lines. The lingering evening sun glinted off the rear window of a car parked off the road on the rutted tracks of an old, disused gravel driveway. He glanced over, and his eyes locked on the car. It was a black, four-door sedan, and Frank caught a glimpse of the license plate as the van whizzed past.

Frank was sure the license plate number started with the letters BLD—the first three letters of the license plate they had almost given up hope of ever finding.

Chapter
9

"THAT'S THE CAR!" Frank exclaimed.

Joe slammed on the brakes.

"Don't stop," Frank told him. "Just slow down a little." He craned his neck out the window, trying to get a better look at the car and the ramshackle house at the end of the driveway.

"Do you know who lives there?" Frank asked Vanessa.

"Nobody," Vanessa said. "The place is abandoned."

"Not anymore," Joe responded, glancing in the rearview mirror.

"What do we do now?" Vanessa asked.

"We take you home," Joe said firmly. "Frank

and I are stuck in the middle of this mess. I don't want you to get tangled up in it, too."

"Oh, that's right," Vanessa responded in a high voice, fluttering her eyelids. "I'm just a poor, defenseless little girl. You big boys will protect me from the bad men."

"Cut it out," Joe grumbled. "That's not what I meant. The Assassins are professional killers. Anybody with any brains would steer clear of them."

"Ah, that explains it," Vanessa said. "It's okay for you to risk your life because you're too dense to know any better."

"We don't have much of a choice," Frank said. "The Assassins are gunning for us, and we have to stop them before they stop us—permanently."

Vanessa sighed. "Do you have to tackle them alone?"

"Who said anything about tackling?" Joe responded as he steered the van down the winding driveway that led to Vanessa's house. "We'll just watch the house and wait for them to make a move."

Vanessa shot him a sidelong glance. "And then what will you do?"

Joe shrugged. "It depends on what they do." He stopped the van in front of the house, reached across the passenger seat, and opened the door.

Vanessa glared at Joe, then got out without uttering another word. Joe sighed and shook his head slowly as he turned the van around and headed back onto the road. "Girls," he muttered. "They want you to take care of everything, *and* they want to take care of everything themselves— all at the same time."

Frank chuckled softly. "You just figured that out now? You've got a long way to go before you can even visit the planet they come from." He picked up the cellular phone and started dialing. "I'm going to call Tony at Mr. Pizza. If Mr. Gray shows up, Tony can tell him where we are."

Joe pulled off the road and hid the van deep in a stand of trees about a hundred yards from the house with the sagging roof and peeling paint with the shiny black sedan parked in front. Frank got the binoculars out of the back of the van, and the two brothers crept to the edge of the trees. They kept a close watch on the house as the soft evening light dwindled and a cloak of darkness covered the fields and woods.

The moon was almost full, casting pale, eerie shadows from the metal framework of the huge electric towers that supported the high-voltage power lines. Joe thought they looked like giant robot skeletons marching across the countryside. One of the towers was less than a hundred feet from the house, and power lines passed directly over the roof.

Joe's gaze shifted to the light in the window of the house. "If that place is supposed to be abandoned, where is the electricity to power the lights coming from? Do you think the Assassins tapped into those overhead power lines?"

Frank chortled. "If they did, they'd blow out every circuit in the house. There are over five hundred thousand volts surging through those cables."

"A half million volts running along a bare wire? That sounds kind of dangerous."

"That's why the lines are strung way up high," Frank explained. "You can't insulate those lines. The shielding would have to be two feet thick."

"No wonder I'm feeling edgy," Joe said. "I think I must be getting zapped by stray electrons."

"It's possible," Frank responded. "But it's more likely that you're just not capable of sitting still for more than about three minutes."

"I hate stakeouts," Joe admitted. "When are we going to get moving?"

The front porch light winked on. Frank scanned the house with the binoculars. "Somebody's coming out." He handed the binoculars to his brother. "Check it out."

It took Joe a second to adjust the focus, and then the face of a man with a thick mustache leapt into view. "That's one of the guys who jumped us at our house!" he whispered.

Frank nodded silently, keeping his eyes trained on the man in front of the house. The terrorist climbed into the black sedan, started the engine, backed the car out of the driveway, and drove off into the night.

"Now we know for sure Assassins were holed up in there," Joe said. "We need to get a closer look to find out if anyone else is there, or if Richards is being held inside."

"Soon," Frank said. He glanced up at the night sky. A thick bank of clouds was rolling in from the west.

As soon as the moving clouds blotted out the pale glow of the moon, the Hardys slipped out of the cover of the woods and darted across the open field. They hugged the shadows and veered around the harsh light spilling out onto the rickety front porch. Joe tried to peek inside the house through a side window, but a heavy curtain completely blocked the view.

Frank and Joe crept around to the back. The rear windows were covered by thick drapes, too, but a thin shaft of bright light streaming out of one window drew the Hardys like a magnet. Crouching under the sill, Joe slowly lifted his head to peer through the space under the shade.

He couldn't see much, but a glimpse of a stove and a sink told him this was the kitchen. He angled his head from side to side to see different parts of the room. His eyes finally focused on a single wooden chair in the middle of the dirty kitchen floor. A man was tied to the chair, his mouth sealed shut with duct tape. Joe instantly recognized the terrified eyes of Oliver Richards and knew this was a man near the end of his rope.

The crunch of tires on gravel caused Joe to jerk away from the window.

"Sounds like our friend is back," Frank whispered. "Did you see anything?"

Joe nodded grimly. "Richards is in there. It looks like he's had a pretty rough time."

"At least he's alive," Frank responded. "Let's get out of here before we end up joining him."

"We can't just leave him in there!" Joe whispered.

"And we can't just burst in and rescue him," Frank insisted. "We don't even know how many people are inside. We need some kind of plan."

Reluctantly Joe followed his brother back to the van hidden in the woods. As they climbed inside, they were startled to discover they weren't alone.

"You've had a busy day," a familiar voice calmly greeted them from the backseat. The plain face of the Gray Man drifted out of the shadows in the back of the van.

"I'm glad you found us," Frank said after he took a deep breath to recover from his shock. "Did you talk to Tony?"

The Gray Man smiled. "I didn't have to. I took the liberty of putting a tap on your phone. I've been monitoring your calls all day."

Frank didn't care much for the sound of that, but he let it pass.

"You were supposed to meet us at Mr. Pizza this afternoon," Joe said. "Where were you?"

"I have to move very carefully," the Gray Man replied. "Every police officer in Bayport is looking for me—not to mention a few Network agents. I thought the car I was driving was safe, untraceable. Apparently I was wrong."

"What happened?" Frank asked.

The Gray Man shrugged. "I ditched the car a couple of miles back."

Joe turned his head to get a better look. "So how did you get here?"

The Gray Man chuckled. "Simple. I walked."

The Hardys told the Gray Man what they had found out, which wasn't much. They didn't know how many Assassins were in the abandoned farmhouse or what was planned for Richards.

"At least they haven't posted any outside guards," the Gray Man noted. "That should work in our favor."

"Guards or no guards," Frank said, "we can't exactly storm the house. The Assassins are probably all carrying automatic weapons, and all we have is a Swiss army knife."

The Gray Man patted the shoulder holster under his gray suit jacket. "Oh, we have a little more than that."

"One pistol won't help much," Frank responded.

"And even if we could match the Assassins' firepower," Joe added, "they could still kill Richards before we got in the front door."

"That's right," Frank agreed. "We have to figure out some way to flush them out of the house without their suspecting anything."

"Hmmm," the Gray Man responded. "That's a tall order." He glanced at his watch. "It's late, and it's been a long day. I suggest we try to get some sleep."

Joe stared at him. "How can you sleep at a time like this?"

The Gray Man sighed. "Until somebody comes up with a better plan, all we can do is sit here and keep an eye on the house, and that job only requires one pair of eyes. We'll take watch in shifts. I'll take the first shift. You boys try to get some rest."

Joe thought he was too keyed up to sleep, but he tried anyway. He closed his eyes for a minute—and the next thing he knew, Frank was shaking him awake.

"Get up," Frank coaxed in a low voice. "It's your turn on watch."

"What time is it?" Joe mumbled, rubbing his eyes.

"A little after four A.M.," Frank told him.

Joe stumbled out of the van and crept to the edge of the woods to get a good view of the house. He enjoyed detective work, but stakeouts were boring. He always found it hard to keep his eyes open and dozed off for a few seconds, only to be startled awake by a rustling in the woods.

He glanced back and spotted a dark shape creeping toward their van. As the figure reached for the door, Joe caught a glimpse of a large weapon clutched in the intruder's other hand. Frank and the Gray Man were sound asleep in the van, Joe realized. Reacting instinctively, he jumped up and bolted toward the van, crashing through the underbrush. The dark figure whirled around, swinging the weapon in Joe's direction.

Joe charged ahead in a desperate attempt to stop the attacker. He knew he was the only thing that stood between his brother and a trained killer.

Chapter

10

JOE GRITTED HIS TEETH and sprinted straight at the shadowy figure. If he could reach the terrorist before the assailant got off a shot, Joe might still have a chance to disarm him. It was a slim chance, but good enough for Joe.

The last twenty feet felt like twenty miles. Joe had a fleeting second to wonder why the intruder hadn't fired. He steeled himself for the gruesome impact of a hail of bullets.

Joe dove low and hit the dark figure with a flying tackle around the knees. The intruder pitched backward with a startled yelp that sounded oddly familiar. Joe grabbed for the weapon still clutched in the intruder's hand. In the same instant that he realized the weapon wasn't a gun, he also got his first good look at his adversary's face. The shock stopped him cold.

"Vanessa?" he sputtered, staring at his girlfriend armed with her bow and quiver of arrows.

"Get off me," she croaked, gasping for air. "You knocked the wind out of me."

Joe helped her sit up and waited for her to catch her breath.

"What are you doing here?" he whispered as he gathered up the arrows scattered on the ground.

"I was worried about you," she said. "I couldn't sleep. I tossed and turned for hours."

"So you decided to take an early morning stroll to check up on us."

Vanessa nodded faintly.

Joe held out the bow he had wrestled away from her in their brief struggle. "And you brought this just in case you ran into any bad guys."

Vanessa snatched the bow out of his hand with an angry swipe. "It was the best I could come up with on short notice. The TV shopping channel had a special deal on bazookas, but they don't offer same-day delivery."

That got a smile out of Joe. "Are you okay? I smashed into you pretty hard."

"Tell me about it," Vanessa responded, bending over to rub her knee. "I used to think it might be fun to play football. Now I know better."

The door of the van creaked open. "What's going on out there?" Frank whispered. He peered out at Vanessa and then looked over at his brother. "I suppose you have an explanation for this."

Joe put his arm around Vanessa. "She came to rescue us."

"How nice," Frank muttered.

"Don't make fun of me," Vanessa retorted, "or I'll take my bow and arrows and go home."

"Is that a promise?" Frank replied.

Vanessa shot him a sharp glance. "Okay, I give up. You win." She looked at the dingy house in the distance. "You probably don't need my help, anyway. If you wait long enough, they'll probably all get sick in there. Then you can just march in and drag them off to jail."

Joe frowned. "What do you mean?"

"Those power lines," Vanessa said, pointing at the thick electric cables hanging high over the sagging roof of the old house. "After the power lines went up, the people who lived there started getting sick all the time. They claimed it had something to do with electromagnetic fields from the high-voltage wires. They tried to sell the place, but nobody was interested, so they moved out, abandoning it."

An idea suddenly struck Frank. "Vanessa," he

said, "could we borrow your bow and a few arrows?"

Vanessa turned to him, a cagey smile on her lips. "Where my bow goes, I go. You can't have one without the other."

"Forget it," Frank said. "It was a stupid idea anyway."

"Stupider than sitting out here all night doing absolutely nothing?" Joe said. "This I have to hear."

"I'd like to hear it, too," the Gray Man added, stepping out of the van. "We have to make a move soon, before the Assassins decide that Mr. Richards has outlived his usefulness."

"All right," Frank said reluctantly. "We need a diversion to flush the Assassins out, right? Well, if we run a wire from the power lines and attach it to the fuse box . . ."

Joe nodded. "That could set off some electrical fireworks inside that might give us the diversion we need."

"It might work," the Gray Man said. "But if the fuse box isn't outside, the plan falls apart."

"There's only one way to find out," Joe responded.

Frank and Joe sneaked back to the house in the early morning light. A shuddering rattle and a loud hum froze them in their tracks. Frank glanced up and spotted a large air conditioner in one of the front upstairs windows.

Joe followed his brother's gaze and realized that the air conditioner must have just kicked on. The machine jutted out so far, it looked as if it might topple out and crash to the ground at any moment.

The Hardys edged around the side of the house to the back. Frank didn't find the fuse box. But what he did find was even better—a metal pipe that ran down the outside wall. At waist level the pipe disappeared into the house. At eye level there was a foot-wide gap in the pipe. A tangle of wires bridged the gap, snaking out from inside the two disconnected ends of the pipe. They were wrapped together with black electrical tape.

"This is where the electric meter was," Frank whispered. "That's how the electric company shuts off the power. They pull the meter and cap the conduit pipes."

"I see the Assassins saved the electric company the trouble of coming all the way out to put in a new meter," Joe remarked. "They reconnected the wires and turned the power back on themselves."

"This makes our job a lot easier," Frank said. He pointed to the jumble of wires. "All we have to do is hook up a line right there."

The Hardys headed back to the van through the cover of the woods. They told Vanessa and the Gray Man about the electric connection.

"So now we know you can tap into the electric power in the house," Vanessa said, "but how are you going to tap into the overhead power lines? They must be at least a hundred feet up."

"That's where your bow comes in," Frank told her.

"I get it," Vanessa replied. "We tie a wire to an arrow and fire it up over the power lines. Right?"

"That's the plan," Frank said.

"Now all we need is a few hundred feet of electric wire," the Gray Man noted.

"Coming right up," Frank responded, climbing into the back of the van. He rummaged around in the tool chest and pawed through a couple of boxes of odds and ends. He emerged with two coils of thin, insulated electric wire.

"I don't think this will make it," Joe observed when they unraveled all the wire. "It's hard to tell for sure, but I'd say we're about twenty feet short."

"No problem," Frank said, picking up the end of one of the wires. "This is speaker wire. It's really two insulated wires stuck together. We can pull it apart down the middle and double the length."

Joe and Vanessa stripped the ends of the insulated lines, twisted the exposed wires together, and wrapped electrical tape around the connections to make one long length of insulated wire.

Frank taped one exposed end to the steel head of an arrow and secured the wire by wrapping electrical tape down the shaft in a tight spiral.

"Okay," the Gray Man said when everything was ready. "Let's go over the plan very carefully. I'll take up a position in the front of the house. With any luck, the Assassins will come out that way when the fireworks start, and I'll get the drop on them."

"Since you have the only gun," Frank noted, "you're our best chance."

"But if anybody comes out the back," Joe said, "we might still have a chance to slip in during the confusion and get Richards out."

"What if nobody comes out at all?" Vanessa asked.

"Then we get out of there as fast as we can," the Gray Man said. He looked over at Frank and Joe. "I mean it. This plan is too risky already. There's no room for any spontaneous heroics."

Vanessa hefted her bow. "Let's get it over with before I realize how crazy this all is."

Joe put his hand on her shoulder. "You're not going," he said. "I can handle the bow."

"I've seen how you handle a bow," Vanessa responded. "I'm ten times better than you, and you know it."

"Accuracy isn't important here," Frank pointed out. "Distance is the critical factor."

"You've done enough already," the Gray Man told Vanessa.

Vanessa sighed and handed the bow to Joe. "I'll wait in the van. Try not to shoot yourself in the foot."

Joe crouched down in the shadow of the house, clutching Vanessa's bow with the arrow nocked in place. Frank attached the wire to the lines running into the house and nodded to his brother. Joe stood up, lifted the bow skyward, drew back the cable as far as it would stretch, and let the arrow fly.

The arrow sailed up into the air, trailing the thin wire behind it. It arced over the high voltage power lines, then fell and jerked to a halt when all the wire was played out. It was now draped over the power lines.

"Stand back," Frank warned his brother in a whisper. Frank used a pair of sticks to reel the wire in slowly, pulling the arrow back up toward the electric cables pulsing with hundreds of thousands of volts. He didn't know what would happen when the steel arrowhead touched the power lines, but he sure wasn't going to be holding the thinly insulated wire with his hands when it happened.

The arrowhead connected with the bare cable in a shower of sparks. Frank dropped the sticks and jumped back, flattening himself against the side of the house next to his brother. More sparks popped and sizzled where the wire was attached to the house lines. Acrid smoke from charred insulation wafted up from the jumble of wires.

A muffled *boom* rang out, followed by a sharp, metallic *crunch* and a chorus of angry shouts.

"It sounds like all the action's up front," Joe said.

"That was the plan, wasn't it?" Frank responded. "Come on, let's get moving."

Frank and Joe rushed to the back door and burst into the kitchen. Richards was alone in the room, still tied to the chair where Joe had seen him the night before. The Hardys quickly untied him and hustled the dazed writer out the back door.

"Frank! Joe!" the Gray Man called out from the other side of the house. "Where are you? Are you all right?"

The Hardys circled around to the front of the house and found the Gray Man with his gun drawn, standing over two men lying facedown on the ground, hands clasped behind their heads.

"There were four of them," the Gray man said. "I managed to stop these two, but the other two got away."

A chill ran down Joe's spine. "Got away? Where did they go?"

"I don't know," the Gray Man answered. "I

THE HARDY BOYS CASEFILES

was sort of busy at the time. Find some rope so
we can tie up these scum."

Joe didn't hear him because he had bolted
across the field and into the woods, his heart
pounding frantically. He skidded to a halt when
he realized the van was gone. Joe's heart sank.
The terrorists had stolen the van—and kidnapped
Vanessa.

Chapter

11

JOE WHIRLED AROUND and sprinted back to the house. If he could hot-wire the Assassins' car, he might be able to catch up to the two who had got away before anything happened to Vanessa. But as he neared the black sedan parked in the driveway, his desperate hope wavered. He now understood the source of the noise he had heard right after a half million volts had blasted the electric system.

The burst of power had blown the air conditioner out of the upstairs window, sending it crashing into the hood and windshield of the car. Joe fought back a sense of despair. He ran to the car and attacked the bulky mass of the air conditioner, wrestling it out of the shattered remnants of the windshield, ignoring the pellets of glass that scratched his hands.

"What's the matter?" Frank asked his brother. "What are you doing?"

"The Assassins have Vanessa!" Joe blurted. "They stole the van! We've got to catch them!"

Joe pulled the massive air conditioner to the edge of the hood and let it crash to the ground. It barely missed his feet.

Frank pulled his brother away from the car with a firm hand. "Get a grip," he said. "We aren't going anywhere in that car."

"We have to!" Joe roared.

"We can't!" Frank shot back. "Take a look at the tires!"

Joe's wild eyes darted down at the ruined, flat tires. "How did that happen?"

The Gray Man cleared his throat. "I slashed the tires earlier so the Assassins couldn't make a getaway."

Joe pounded the hood with his fist. "We have to get a car somewhere!"

"We will," the Gray Man assured him. "And we'll do whatever it takes to get Vanessa back. That's a promise."

Oliver Richards emerged from the deserted house with the rope the terrorists had used on him. "This should hold our friends for a while."

"Tie them up nice and tight," the Gray Man instructed. "We don't want them to slip away before they've had a long chat with some of my former colleagues."

Frank looked at the outlaw agent. "You're going to turn them over to the Network?"

The Gray Man shrugged. "The only other alternative is the Bayport police, and I don't think Chief Collig knows the proper questions to ask international terrorists."

Richards made the hike to the closest phone seem much longer because he couldn't stop talking.

"Those guys were really tough," the writer prattled on. "They kept me tied up all the time. They didn't give me any food. They wouldn't even let me go to the bathroom. Who are they, anyway?"

"Assassins," Frank answered.

"Hired killers, huh? Who do they work for?"

"They work for themselves," Frank said. "Didn't you know that? How much do you know about the Assassins?"

"Are you telling me that's the *name* of a terrorist group?" Richards asked. "I never came across it in any of my research."

Joe stopped and looked at the writer. "You never heard of the Assassins? You don't know anything about the Assassins or the Network?"

"The Network?" Richards responded. "Is that a rival terrorist group? Are we caught in the middle of some international criminal underworld turf war?" The idea seemed to cheer him up. "Wow, what a great story this will make!"

They stopped at a gas station, and the Gray Man made two quick phone calls—the first to a cab company.

"Is the Network going to pick up those guys we left tied up back at the house?" Frank asked him after the second call.

The Gray Man snorted. "They'd never pass up a chance to question a pair of Assassins."

"We're wasting time," Joe grumbled. "We need to track down the Assassins who have Vanessa."

"Why didn't we just call the police?" Richards ventured.

"You don't get it, do you?" Joe snapped. "The police would just turn the whole case over to the Network. And by the time they acted it would be too late!"

Richards nodded thoughtfully. "I see. So it's all up to us. Well, we outsmarted those terrorists once, and we can do it again."

Joe stared at the writer. " 'We'? What did *you* do? Let's see— Oh, yeah, you cleverly lit a fire under half the terrorists in the country, dragged us into the middle of them, and then got yourself abducted by an international gang of professional killers!"

"Give me a break. All I did was write a novel."

"And that's *all* you're going to do," the Gray Man responded. "Keep a low profile for a while, stay away from spy stories, and you probably won't have any more trouble."

"What is this?" Richards retorted. "Some kind of brush-off? You guys can't ditch me now. The story's just starting to get interesting."

He turned from the Gray Man's impassive face to the Hardys. "Come on, guys," he pleaded. "Give me a chance. After what those sleazebags did to me, I want to get them as badly as you do. I can help. I know I can."

"The only help we need right now is wheels," Joe said. "So unless you can write a car into this story line, take a hike."

"Your friends seem reliable," the Gray Man said to the Hardys. "Could we have the cab take us to one of their houses to borrow a car?"

Joe shook his head forcefully. "I don't want to drag any of them into this—not after what happened to Vanessa."

"Joe's right," Frank said. "We're on our own."

"What about my car?" Richards spoke up.

Joe shot a sidelong glance at the writer. "Are you still here?"

Richards smiled. "You need wheels. I have wheels. If we all work together, my car is your car."

"There's only one small hitch," Frank said. "After we told the police you were kidnapped, they probably seized your car as evidence."

Richards's smile faltered and then widened

again as he reached into his back pocket. "It's a good thing those Assassins are terrorists, not muggers," he said. He pulled out his wallet and flashed a credit card. "And it's a good thing we live in a country where you can buy just about anything you want even if you don't have the money to pay for it."

Joe was surprised at how fast and easy it was to buy a car—if you paid full sticker price in cash. Richards's credit card wasn't exactly cash, but it was good enough for the dealer. He smiled and waved as Richards steered the dented, rust-blotched vehicle, which belched a trail of blue smoke, out of the used-car lot.

"Is this the best you could do?" Joe complained from the cramped backseat of the once bright yellow, two-door sedan.

"This car is a classic," Richards responded cheerfully. "You don't see many 1965 GTOs on the road anymore."

"It's an antique," Joe muttered.

"It'll do zero to sixty in under seven seconds," the writer claimed a little defensively.

"It won't do zero to sixty in seven *minutes* if the engine isn't tuned right," Joe retorted. "And I'll bet this beater hasn't had a tune-up in my lifetime."

"Uh-oh," Richards murmured, staring at the road ahead. "There's a police car in the other lane up at the stoplight. We're going to pull up right next to him."

"Slow down," Frank advised. "Maybe the light will change before we get there."

Richards slowed to a crawl, but the stubborn traffic light was still red when he rumbled up next to the police squad car. There were two uniformed officers in the car. Frank didn't recognize either of them. The one in the passenger seat glanced over at the beat-up old car.

The Gray Man melted into the seat next to Richards.

"Hey," the police officer called out the window. "Isn't that a '65 GTO?"

Richards gave a jerky nod. "Uh, yeah."

The police officer gave the car an appraising eye. "You should take better care of it. That car is a classic."

"Uh, yeah, I know," Richards responded.

"Does it have the dual-quad carburetors?"

"Ah, gee, I don't know."

The police officer frowned. "You don't know?" He peered closely at the writer. "You seem a little nervous, fella. What's the problem?"

He squinted into the car, and his eyes widened when he saw the Gray Man. "I know you!" he exclaimed, pointing a finger at the man. The police officer jumped out of the police car and whipped out his service revolver. "Everybody out of the car, now!"

Chapter

12

"GET OUT OF THE CAR with your hands on your heads!" the police officer bellowed.

Richards stared at the man's drawn gun, transfixed.

"We're unarmed!" Frank called out. Then he remembered the Gray Man's pistol but decided not to mention it. The cop had already worked himself into a frenzy. A twitch of his trigger finger could be fatal. No one moved to get out.

Joe groaned. "That's it. It's over."

"Take it easy, Officer," the Gray Man said in a calm voice that rang with authority. "We won't make any trouble."

In the rearview mirror, Joe saw a strange look in Richards's eyes.

"I said get out of the car!" the cop barked. "You're all under arrest."

"You'll have to catch us first!" Richards suddenly yelled, flooring the gas pedal.

"Are you nuts?" Frank burst out as the rusted muscle car squealed away from the light and blasted across the intersection. "That cop could have blown your head off!"

Richards shook his head. "Standard police regulations prohibit the use of firearms against unarmed suspects who don't pose an immediate physical threat—and that includes suspects who are escaping."

"Police officers have been known to forget regulations in the heat of the moment," the Gray Man noted dryly, grabbing the armrest as the car screeched around a corner. "You took a big risk back there."

"Yeah," Richards responded, clutching the steering wheel in a two-fisted grip. "Well, that's what this job is all about, isn't it? You have to take a few risks now and then. Where's your sense of adventure?"

"Right next to my sense of proportion," the Gray Man answered. "Every police car in Bayport will be joining the chase before long."

"What do you want me to do?" Richards snapped. "Stop the car and wait for them to catch us?"

"No!" Joe blurted out. He glanced out the rear

window and saw a blue light flashing in the distance. "We might be able to shake them off. We've gone this far. Let's ride it out."

Frank looked over at his brother's strained features. The Hardys' first clash with the Assassins had ended in Joe's girlfriend, Iola Morton, being killed when a bomb placed by the terrorists ripped apart the Hardys' car. Frank knew that Joe would stop at nothing to make sure history didn't repeat itself. Frank had to stand by his brother—all the way.

"Turn left up here," Frank told Richards. "There's a deserted warehouse a few blocks down. We can hide the car there."

"Richards and I will have to stay out of sight, too," the Gray Man said. "Every cop in town has seen my picture, and that officer got a good look at Richards."

"We'll get another car somewhere and try to pick up the Assassins' trail," Joe said. He suddenly groaned and slapped his forehead. "The cellular phone in the van— If we could talk to them, maybe we could convince them to release Vanessa."

"You'd have to be very convincing," the Gray Man responded. "Right now, Vanessa's life depends on her value as a hostage. What would make the Assassins let her go?"

"I don't know!" Joe snapped. "A trade, maybe. I'll offer myself in her place," he added hastily.

"Uh-oh," Richards said. "It looks as if the warehouse is out of the question."

Joe glanced out the windshield and saw a cruiser speeding toward them, lights flashing and siren wailing. "Do something!" he shouted.

Richards slammed on the brakes, jammed the gearshift into reverse, and punched the gas. The tires screamed and smoked as the car flew backward down the pavement.

"Look out!" Frank shouted, staring out the rear window. Another police car careened onto the street behind them, cutting off their escape.

Richard hit the brakes again, and the car screeched to a halt.

Joe glanced frantically from police car to police car that had them sandwiched in a trap.

"We can make a run for it," he insisted, reaching for the door handle.

Frank grabbed his brother's shoulder. "Running won't help Vanessa. How can we track down the Assassins while we're running and hiding from the police?"

Joe buried his head in his hands. "What are we going to do?"

"Tell them everything," the Gray Man said, "and hope somebody believes us before it's too late."

Two more cruisers and a couple of unmarked cars converged on the scene as the Hardys got out of the car after the writer and Mr. Gray. All four of them held their hands up high, acutely aware that they were surrounded by a wall of deadly firepower.

"Turn around slowly and put your hands on the hood of the car!" one of the officers ordered.

Frank and Joe did what they were told and waited for the police to handcuff them and haul them off to jail. There was an urgent murmur of voices behind them. Frank risked a quick peek and spotted the two Network agents who had dragged Richards out of the pizza restaurant.

The agents were talking to one of the uniformed officers. The agents' faces remained rigid, impassive, but Frank could tell from the police officer's angry gestures that some kind of argument was going on. Two more unmarked cars pulled up. Police Chief Collig got out of one car, and a slim man with thick glasses stepped out of the backseat of the other car.

Chief Collig looked harried and grumpy. His uniform was rumpled. In contrast, the man in the glasses was dressed for corporate success in a perfectly pressed, dark gray pinstripe suit. This odd couple stepped into the middle of the whispered argument. When the man with the thick glasses talked, everybody else listened.

When the debate was over, the three nonpolice personnel emerged from the cluster of uniforms and walked over to the rusted yellow sedan.

"You gave us quite a chase, Mr. Gray," the

man in the glasses said. He gave the Gray Man a curt nod and then turned to the writer with a smile. "I'm glad to see you're safe and unharmed. We were quite worried about you. I read part of your new book. It's really very fascinating."

"I'm always glad to hear that people enjoy my work," Richards replied.

"I didn't say I enjoyed it," the man responded. His cool gaze shifted to Frank and Joe. "And you must be the famous Hardy brothers I've heard so much about. You've been busy the last few days, haven't you?"

"We need to talk to the guy in charge," Joe said bluntly. "If it's not you, then go get him. We don't have much time."

"This is Mr. Henkels," the Gray Man spoke up. "If anybody's in charge here, he's the man."

"So what is it you need to tell me?" Henkels asked Joe.

"Mr. Gray had nothing to do with Richards's abduction. The Assassins did it, and now they have my girlfriend, Vanessa Bender. They're in a black van, license plate num—"

"We know all about that," Henkels cut in, "and we're working on it." He turned to the Gray Man. "That was quite a gift you left for us out at the old farmhouse. We managed to get enough information to figure out what's going on."

"Does that mean I'm clear now?" the Gray Man responded.

The man in the thick glasses nodded, and barely moving his lips, said, "I guess I owe you an apology. But before I do—apologize, that is— you can tell me how an innocent young woman fell into the hands of the Assassins."

The Gray Man stiffened.

"That's not important right now," Frank spoke up. Henkels bristled. "Getting her back is our only concern," Frank continued.

"There's a cellular phone in the van," Joe said. "We could contact the Assassins and try to work out a deal. You know, negotiate some kind of—"

"We don't negotiate with terrorists," Henkels said in a monotone. "We know how to handle this kind of situation. I know you are trying to help, but stay out of the way now—please."

Joe took a step toward the man in glasses, fists clenched, glaring angrily. A human tank in a suit stepped between them.

"He's right, Joe," Frank said quickly. He glanced around the bulk of the Network agent. "Are we free to go?"

Henkels waved a hand in a single gesture, and the Network agent moved out of the way. "Of course," he said in a dismissive tone.

Frank glanced at the Gray Man. "Mr. Gray?"

"I'll stay," he replied.

"I'd like to stick around, too, if you don't mind," Richards spoke up.

"I *do* mind," Henkels said. "Do you have a problem with that?" he asked without blinking.

Richards turned to the Hardys and with a forced smile asked, "Can I give you a lift?"

Joe made Richards stop at the first phone booth they passed. He wouldn't let anyone stand in his way when Vanessa's life was on the line.

Frank knew what Joe was going to do, and also knew he would have done exactly the same thing.

Joe punched in the number of their van phone and let it ring twenty times before he hung up. He tried two more times. On the third try, somebody answered. "What do you want?" a harsh voice growled.

"We want to make a trade," Joe replied, his heart pounding. "Let the girl go and take me instead."

"An interesting offer," the voice on the phone replied. "Who are you?"

"Joe Hardy. Maybe you've heard of me?"

A callous laugh answered Joe's question. "Not good enough. We want the Gray Man. If you can't deliver him, the girl dies."

Chapter

13

JOE LISTENED while the Assassin issued instructions. Before he could respond, the phone line went dead.

Joe reluctantly hung up the pay phone, a dreadful sense of doom overwhelming him. "They want the Gray Man," he informed his brother in a flat voice. "If they don't get him, they'll kill Vanessa."

"Where and when?" Frank prodded gently.

"The state park in an hour," Joe said.

"That doesn't give us much time to work out a plan," Frank admitted. "But we'll come up with something."

"Where is this park?" Richards asked.

"About twenty miles south of town," Frank said.

"Then we'll have to come up with something fast," the writer responded. "It'll take half an hour just to get there."

The brown sedan pulled up next to the pay phone, and Joe saw the two Network agents. Their bulk blocked Joe's view of the lone passenger in the backseat. The back door swung open, and the Gray Man stepped out.

"Mind if I join you?" he asked with a slight smile. Without waiting for an answer, he turned and uttered a few words to the men in the car. They drove off.

Mixed emotions churned inside Joe. The key to Vanessa's release was standing right in front of him, but how could he possibly ask the Gray Man to sacrifice himself? Then another thought struck him.

"Were you sent to keep an eye on us?" Joe asked warily.

The Gray Man shook his head. "I had a sudden urge to take a vacation. Officially, I'm not working. I'm just a tourist looking for excitement. Do you know where I could find some?"

"You don't want to know," Joe said.

The Gray Man studied Joe's face carefully. "Something tells me you've already made contact with our friends. What's the deal?"

"The Assassins want you in exchange for the girl," Richards told him.

The Gray Man pursed his lips. "I see. Well, I

got her into this mess. This is my chance to get her out. How do we make the trade?"

"We can't ask you to do this," Joe said. "The Assassins want your head on a platter."

"They want what's *inside* my head more," the Gray Man responded. "I can string them along for a while and buy some time. Who knows? I might even find a way to escape."

"There's almost no chance of that, and you know it," Frank said.

"It's better than the chance Vanessa has if we don't go for the deal," the Gray Man replied.

"We can't trust those guys," Richards argued. "They might kill the girl no matter what we do."

"They'll have to kill me first," Joe vowed grimly.

"We need some kind of plan," Frank said. "If we don't watch every step we make, we could all end up dead."

"That's why I'm going in alone," the Gray Man announced.

"Not a chance," Joe said. "I have to be there."

"Where Joe goes, I go," Frank added.

Richards dangled the car keys in his hand. "You'll have a long walk without me."

They all piled into the car, and Richards fired up the 350-horsepower dynamo under the hood. "They sure don't make them like this anymore," he said wistfully. The overpowered engine rumbled. The whole car shuddered. Then the engine coughed once and died.

"No, they sure don't," Joe snapped. "Nowadays they make cars that actually go someplace."

Again Richards turned the key in the ignition. The engine sputtered before settling into a throaty growl. "That's more like it," he said with a smile.

Frank glanced at his watch. "We don't have much time. The deadline is forty minutes from now."

"Hang on," Richards responded, punching the gas pedal and peeling away from the curb. "We'll get there in time for the party." He paused for a second. "There's just one thing I have to know."

"What's that?" Joe responded.

"How do I get there?"

Joe directed Richards to the road that would take them to the state park. The rusting muscle car roared onto the four-lane highway. At sixty miles an hour, the engine almost purred.

Richards patted the dashboard. "This baby was built for speed. She belongs out here on the open road."

"What time is it?" Joe asked anxiously.

"We still have almost half an hour," Frank said. "It's a straight shot south on the expressway. We should make it with a few minutes to spare."

Fifteen miles outside Bayport, Joe spotted a

road sign that announced the exit for the state park was five miles ahead.

"Uh-oh," Richard murmured, frowning and tapping the instrument panel. "The temperature gauge is in the red. I don't know how much farther we can get before the engine overheats."

Joe leaned over and peered at the gauge. The needle was more than simply in the red zone—it was almost off the scale. "This car is old," he said, not wanting to acknowledge the problem. "The temperature gauge is probably broken."

Smoke started billowing from the hood.

"I don't think so," Richards said, pulling over to the side of the road.

"We can't stop now!" Joe protested.

"We won't make it another mile before we blow out the engine," the writer insisted.

Joe took a deep breath and forced himself to calm down before getting out. "Okay. Let's see what the trouble is. Maybe we can fix it."

More smoke billowed out when Joe popped the hood. "It's just steam," he said, waving his hands to clear the air. He pointed to a thin stream of vapor hissing out of a black hose. "There's a crack in the water hose. Is there tape or anything to seal it with?"

"I'll check the trunk," Richards said.

Frank unscrewed the radiator cap and squinted down inside. "We're going to need some water, too."

116

"One thing at a time," Joe muttered, wiping the hose dry with his shirtsleeve.

The trunk slammed shut, and Richards returned, holding out a dirty rag. "This is all I could find."

"We need more than that," Joe said. "What we really need is some hose tape or duct tape. But if we had something like putty that we could use to seal the crack ..."

"Something like gum?" the Gray Man ventured.

"Exactly," Joe said, looking at the Network agent hopefully. "Do you have some?"

"I'm afraid not," the Gray Man answered.

Joe's disappointment was written all over his face.

Richards patted his shirt and pants and reached into a pocket. "But I do," he declared, beaming as he pulled out a pack of gum.

Joe snatched the gum out of the writer's hand and ripped the pack open. "Chew as fast as you can," he ordered, handing everybody a stick of gum.

Two minutes later Joe smeared a gooey wad of gum along the leaky hose. Then he wrapped the rag around the hose and tied it in a tight knot. "That should hold it for a while," he said.

"We still need water," Frank pointed out.

"Coming right up," Joe replied, checking the level of the windshield washer fluid reservoir.

"Looks like this is plain water in here, and there's plenty of it," he said.

"Good idea," Frank responded. "But how do we get it out of there and into the radiator?"

"No problem," Joe said. "Let me have your knife for a minute."

Frank handed over his pocketknife. Joe took hold of the thin plastic hose that led to the windshield and cut it about three feet from the washer fluid container. Then he stuck the severed end of the hose into the open radiator.

"Crank her up and hit the windshield washer switch," Joe told Richards. "We're going to pump the washer fluid into the radiator—and we're not going to stop again even if a horde of locusts splatters the windshield so we can't see."

The GTO hit the exit ramp for the state park, going a bit over the limit. Joe prayed there weren't any cops in the area. If a state trooper stopped them now, that would be the end for Vanessa.

Richards drove like a demon and almost missed the park entrance. He had to slam on the brakes and swerve at the main gate. They all smiled and acted nonchalant as Richards forked over three dollars to a park ranger for the daily fee, and then Richards took off again. Joe told Richards to stop at a side road blocked off by a swinging metal gate.

"Take this road," Joe said, climbing out of the car. "That's what the guy on the phone told me." He ran over to the gate and was relieved to discover that it was unlocked. He pushed the gate open, waved the car ahead, then jumped back in as it rolled past.

They found the van in a small deserted parking area deep in the woods. They stopped and waited, not sure what to do next. A tense minute ticked by, and then another.

"It looks like it's up to us to make the first move," the Gray Man finally said. He asked Joe to step out so he could push the seat up and get out.

"Wait," Frank said, joining them. "What are you going to do?"

The Gray Man nodded toward the van. "I'm going to walk over there and give the Assassins what they want."

"You're not doing anything until we're sure Vanessa is safe," Joe insisted. "Hey!" he shouted to the van. "Let's see the girl! This deal won't go down until we see her!"

There was no response from the van.

The Gray Man broke away from the Hardys and, holding his hands over his head, moved toward the van. "I'm coming over!" he called out. "Release the girl! I'm the one you want."

A gunshot rang out, piercing the ominous silence. The Gray Man halted in midstride. Joe held his breath. Frank heard a rustling noise in the woods behind them and whirled around. A dozen men in camouflage gear burst into the clearing, clutching assault weapons.

"Nobody move!" a voice blared over a bullhorn. "You are surrounded by federal agents! Come out with your hands up!"

"No!" Joe cried out. "You can't do this! They'll kill—"

Joe's voice was drowned out by a deafening explosion, and then the breath was sucked out of his lungs as the van burst into flames. He relived the moment when another ball of heat and flame had taken the life of his girlfriend Iola Morton.

Chapter

14

"No!" Joe screamed, running toward the in-ferno that consumed the shell of the van. The Assassins had done it again—snuffed out the life of someone close to the Hardys—and once again the brothers could do nothing but watch in horror.

Frank bolted after Joe and snagged his arm. "Stay back!" he shouted, tugging on his brother. "There's nothing you can do. Nobody could have survived that blast."

Joe jerked his arm free, stumbled forward a few feet, and fell to his knees. "Not again," he moaned, staring at the flames.

Frank felt his brother's pain. He, too, still had nightmarish memories of Iola's death. And now

Vanessa was gone, too, and the skeleton of their van stood as a haunting reminder of the past.

Frank tried to help his brother up, but Joe pushed him away. Then Joe heard a voice that brought him to his feet, eyes blazing.

"Get these people out of here!" Henkels ordered in a stern voice. "Clear the area!"

Joe stormed over to the man in the thick glasses. "You're the one who did this," Joe raved. "You're responsible. You knew the Assassins would never surrender."

"He *should* have known," the Gray Man said, stepping between Joe and Henkels.

"Were you in on it, too?" Joe snarled. "Was this all a setup?"

"I knew nothing about it," the Gray Man said, and put a hand on Joe's shoulder. "If I had, I would have done everything I could to stop it."

Frank and Richards flanked Joe on either side, all their eyes on Henkels.

"My men didn't blow up the van," Henkels said curtly. "There will be an investigation."

"How did you know we were meeting the Assassins here?" Frank asked.

The Gray Man grimaced. "I think I know. They must have searched my car after I ditched it. The gear I used to tap your cellular phone was in my car."

Henkels nodded. "When you called the Assassins on the mobile phone, I picked up the conversation loud and clear."

"Sir!" a voice called out. "You'd better take a look at this." Frank glanced over his shoulder. A team of agents was already sifting through the smoking wreckage.

Henkels squared his shoulders and moved to join his men.

"What's that noise?" Richards asked.

"What noise?" Joe responded. Then he heard it. There was a faint, electronic chirrup coming from a nearby clump of bushes.

Richards waded into the bushes, stooped down, and picked something up. "It's a telephone!" he announced. The phone chirruped again, and Richards answered it. "Hello? Hold on a second." He came out of the bushes and handed the cellular phone to Joe. "It's for you."

"I hope I didn't catch you at a bad time," a man on the phone said. Joe couldn't place the voice, but he was sure he had heard it before. "I understand you recently suffered a tragic loss."

"Who is this?" Joe asked sharply.

"Who I am is not nearly as important as who I have," the man replied. "And she would like to talk to you."

There was a slight pause, and then Joe heard a voice that he thought had been silenced forever.

"Joe? Are you there?" The girl on the phone was hesitant, unsure, but Joe had no doubts.

"Vanessa!" he exclaimed. "I thought you were dead! Are you okay?"

"Well, *okay* isn't exactly how I'd describe it," Vanessa replied. "But I should be all right as long as I don't drink the water up here."

"The water?" Joe responded, puzzled. "What do you—"

"We knew the Network would never hand over the Gray Man," the man with the strangely familiar voice cut in. "Did you enjoy the surprise package we left for you in the middle of their pathetic trap? What happened to your van was just a warning of what could happen to your girlfriend. Do you understand, Joseph?"

Joe finally placed the voice. He would never forget the case in which he and Frank had trailed this Assassin, who called himself Bob, from Alaska all the way to Southeast Asia. "What do you want, Bob?"

"You thought you could forget all about me after you left me to rot in a cell in Indonesia," the terrorist said.

"You played a rough game, and you lost," Joe said. "What did you expect when you got caught? A medal and a ticker tape parade?"

"I didn't expect to be betrayed by a young man I recruited into our secret brotherhood," the Assassin replied flatly. "I should have killed you when we captured you in Alaska."

"Is that what this is all about?" Joe asked.

"You were upset because we stopped you before you could drop a hydrogen bomb down a volcano and rip the planet apart? So now you want revenge?"

The man on the phone chuckled dryly. "Come now, Joseph. I'm a professional. This is just business, and a good businessman always has an insurance plan. Your girlfriend is our insurance. If all goes according to plan, she will be released unharmed."

"When?" Joe responded.

"When our business is complete," the Assassin answered.

The line went dead, and Joe was left staring at the phone.

"Was that the Assassins?" Henkels demanded, storming over and snatching the phone.

Joe nodded. "The guy's code name is Bob. We've run into him before."

"The Assassin we chased from Alaska to Indonesia?" Frank responded.

"Wow," Richards said. "This sounds more exotic than anything I could have dreamed up." He pulled out a pocket notebook and started scribbling. "I've got to start writing this stuff down."

"Bob must have escaped from prison," the Gray Man said. "After we broke up the Assassins' scheme to detonate a nuclear bomb along a major fault line in the Pacific Ocean, the Indonesian government locked him up and threw away the key."

"The Assassins still have the girl, don't they?" Henkels said.

"How did you know that?" Frank asked.

"There aren't any bodies in the wreckage," Henkels answered. "The bomb was either on a timer, or they triggered it by remote control." He turned his full attention to Joe. "Now, tell me everything this Bob said."

After Joe related his brief conversation with the Assassin, Henkels strongly advised the Hardys and Richards to go home and stay there until the Assassins were caught. Richards gave the Hardys a ride home, and the Gray Man rode along. The Network agents in the dull brown sedan stayed on the tail of the bright yellow muscle car until Richards pulled into the Hardys' driveway. That was their "escort" to make sure there weren't any unscheduled detours.

"We've got to figure out what the Assassins are up to," Joe said as soon as they were in the house.

"It's fairly clear they don't really want the Gray Man," Frank responded. "That setup at the state park was just a diversion."

"The Assassins must be planning something," the Gray Man said. "And whatever it is, it's going to happen soon. Why else would they want a hostage for 'insurance'?"

"Maybe they just want to make sure they've

escaped the Network dragnet before they release her," Richards ventured.

The Gray Man shook his head. "The Assassins don't need a hostage for that. I've lost count of the times they've just slipped through my fingers. Trying to catch them is like trying to hold water in your bare hands."

The Gray Man's words echoed in Joe's head, and then he heard Vanessa's voice again. "Vanessa was trying to tell me something on the phone," he said, pacing back and forth across the living room. "She made this weird crack about not drinking the water."

"That reminds me of a conversation I overheard when the Assassins had me tied up in that old farmhouse," Richards replied. "I didn't catch very much, but one of them mentioned something about 'New Yorkers getting a taste of Assassin medicine.'"

Frank watched as the pieces of the puzzle started falling into place. "Wait a second," he murmured.

Joe turned to his brother. "What is it?"

"I'm not sure," Frank responded. "I have to use the computer to get more information." He looked at the Gray Man. "I may need your help with some security codes."

An hour later Frank was staring at the cold, hard facts. "Plutonium from dismantled warheads isn't the only nuclear material at the Rocky Mountain Arsenal," he told the others clustered around the computer screen. "All those years of making bombs created a huge amount of radioactive waste. For a while the plant operators dumped the toxic gunk in open pits. When they were forced to dredge the holding pits, they loaded the sludge into barrels."

"I'm sure the Environmental Protection Agency would be fascinated by all this," Joe remarked. "But what does it have to do with the Assassins or the Network?"

"Most of the radioactive waste is still right there at the plant," Frank explained. "The barrels are stored in a minimum security area far from the main buildings. The stuff is so poisonous, nobody ever figured anyone would be crazy enough to steal it."

"The Assassins are crazy enough," Joe realized.

Frank nodded. "And the security logs from the plant's computer system indicate several minor breaches of the outside perimeter in the past few weeks."

Richards frowned. "I don't get it. Why would they want to steal radioactive waste?"

"To threaten the lives of seven or eight million people," Frank said grimly. "They want to poison the New York City water supply."

Chapter

15

"WE HAVE TO STOP the Assassins," Frank said. "A few dozen barrels of radioactive waste could turn the New York City water supply into deadly poison."

"How do you know that's their plan?" asked Richards, notebook in hand as usual.

"Okay, here's the logic," Frank explained. "Put together Vanessa's comment about not drinking the water with what you overheard them saying about giving New Yorkers a taste of their medicine. Add the fact that they probably got hold of a load of radioactive material out in Colorado, and it would follow that they are going to use stuff to blackmail the city."

"Hold on a second," Richards spoke up. "How

are the Assassins going to get the toxic gunk into the city's water supply?"

"Good question," Frank replied. "If we can figure out how they plan to do it, that might tell us where it will happen."

"I think I know," Joe said. "All the city's water has to go through a filtration plant for cleaning. There's a water filtration plant about halfway between Bayport and New York. Half the water in the city is probably pumped through that plant."

"That must be the place where the Assassins plan to strike," the Gray Man concluded. He picked up the phone on Frank's desk and punched in a number.

"What are you doing?" Joe asked.

"I'm contacting the Network," the Gray Man said.

Joe yanked the phone out of his hand. "You can't do that! What about Vanessa? The Network doesn't care about her!"

The Gray Man's steady gaze bore into Joe's. "I'm sorry Vanessa is caught in the middle," he said, "but millions of lives are at stake here." He slowly pried the phone out of Joe's rigid hand. "That's why I have to alert the Network."

"You know he's right," Frank said as they watched the Gray Man leave the house and get into a car the Network had sent for him.

Joe turned to his brother. "I don't know anything anymore. What are we supposed to do now? Sit around watching TV until it's over?"

"You know," Richards ventured, "it's possible that nothing will happen. Everything hinges on a few hints, a couple of educated guesses. *Maybe* the Assassins stole radioactive waste from the Rocky Mountain Arsenal. *Maybe* they want to poison the New York water supply. *Maybe* they plan to do it by dumping the stuff in the water at the filtration plant."

"That last point's been bothering me," Frank said. "The filtration plant seems like a logical spot—but is it the only one?"

"More important," Richards added, "is it the best? A city the size of New York uses a lot of water," he mused. "Where does it all come from?"

"I read about that once," Frank responded, racking his brain to recall the facts. "There are a series of reservoirs up north in the mountains."

"Up north?" Joe echoed. "In the mountains?" Vanessa's exact words boomed in his skull, and he clutched his brother's arm. "Vanessa said 'the water *up here*'! That could mean north or in the mountains!"

"Or both," Richards noted. "I'll bet it's a lot easier to get into one of those reservoirs than into a water filtration plant."

Joe got out a road atlas and flipped to the map

of New York State. "Look at this," he said. "The reservoirs are marked as state parks."

"That's right," Frank said. "I remember now. The reservoirs are manmade lakes. There was a big debate over public access to the lakes. The state has pretty strict limits on the number of people they let in each year—but basically all you need is a camping permit."

Richards's eyes lit up. "Do you have a tent? I'm suddenly in the mood for a taste of the outdoor life."

"Sounds good to me," Joe said. "Let's do it."

"Not so fast," Frank responded, scanning the map. "There are a lot of reservoirs. We can't check them all. "We need to narrow it down. He focused on a symbol near one of the reservoirs. The symbol was the shape of a tiny airplane. "Check this out," he said, tapping the marker with his finger. "This is a regional airport."

"So?" Richards responded. "Are we going to fly there?"

"No," Frank replied. "But Bob could."

"He sure could," Joe agreed. "He flew choppers for the Assassins in the Alaskan wilderness. I remember him skimming along the treetops at full throttle, ducking under the military radar. He could fly just about anything."

"How far is that reservoir from here?" Richards asked.

Frank studied the distance on the map, then

said, "If we leave now, we can be there first thing in the morning."

They took turns driving through the night. When Joe wasn't behind the wheel, he either stared out into the blackness or dozed off for a few minutes at a time. He was driving when they reached the turnoff for the reservoir at first light.

"This is it," Joe said, nudging his brother awake.

Frank rubbed his eyes and checked the road map. "The airport's a few miles farther up the road. Let's check that out first."

"Why?" Joe asked. "If the reservoir is the Assassins' target, that's where they'll show up."

"That's true," Frank conceded. "But if they aren't there already, it'd be better to get to them before they haul that stuff anywhere near the water."

"And the airport's a lot smaller than the reservoir," Richards spoke up. "It'll be easier to search."

Joe followed the road signs to the airport. A small prop plane taxied along a runway and buzzed off into the sunrise. A few cars were scattered about the parking lot. Joe parked near the air traffic control tower, and they all got out and stretched their legs.

Frank scanned the handful of aircraft hangars and the planes that clustered around them. Most of them were single-engine propeller planes—the kind Frank had trained in when he got his pilot's license. There were a few two-engine planes and a lone jet that looked as if it could hold six passengers.

"Well, this shouldn't take long," Frank remarked. "Let's take a look around and see what we can find."

"What are we looking for?" Joe responded. "A plane with the Assassins' logo on it?"

Richards chuckled. "That would be something, wouldn't it?" A thoughtful look crossed his face. "Hmm—I wonder what it would look like. How about a python coiled around the barrel of a submachine gun? Or a bloody dagger piercing the planet. Boy, that would make a great book cover."

Frank and Joe both stared at him.

Richards shrugged. "Sorry. I get carried away sometimes."

They nosed around the first few hangars without finding anything of interest. Frank started into the gloomy interior of the next hangar and sucked in his breath.

An air-sea cargo plane with a pair of overhead engines lurked in the deep shadows. They slipped into the dark hangar and padded over to the plane. Joe tried the cargo door and discovered it was unlocked. Enough sunlight seeped into the hangar to reveal the contents of the plane.

"It's empty," Joe said, disappointment clear in his voice.

Frank climbed inside the plane. "Let's take a closer look. If this is the Assassins' plane, we might find some kind of clue that will lead us to them."

"Sure," Joe muttered. "Maybe they left us a note. 'Gone to blow up a hospital and burn an orphanage. Back in a half hour.'" Despite his words, Joe still clung to a thin strand of hope and joined his brother and the writer in the search.

It didn't take long to comb the sparse interior of the cargo hold. Frank found a baggage compartment in the rear, but it was empty, too. "I'm going to check the cockpit," he said, moving forward. "Then we'll—" He stopped and cocked his head.

A faint rumbling outside grew louder, closer. It sounded like a truck. Before long, its engine was idling right outside the hangar. A metallic creak and a growing shaft of sunlight told Frank that somebody was pushing open the wide hangar doors. Frank motioned his brother and the writer back into the shadows in the rear of the plane, and he flattened himself against the wall next to the cargo hatch.

The deep thrum of a diesel engine filled the hangar as the truck rolled inside. The sound abruptly stopped. Frank heard one door slam and then another.

A quick glimpse out at the new arrivals confirmed Frank's fears. The Assassin known as Bob climbed out of the truck.

"Let's load up," Bob instructed another Assassin—the scowling man with the bushy mustache who had escaped when the Hardys rescued Richards. The two terrorists moved around to the back of the truck, and Frank slipped away from the cargo door and back toward the rear of the plane.

"They're about to load the plane," he whispered, opening the hatch to the baggage compartment. "We've got to hide."

Joe peered inside the low, cramped space. "There's not enough room for all of us in there."

"We'll *make* room," Frank responded, pushing his brother inside. Richards crawled in behind Joe, and Frank squeezed in last. They were jammed in so tightly that he couldn't shut the hatch all the way. He pulled it closed as far as he could and held it tightly, praying the Assassins wouldn't notice.

The plane shook and swayed as the terrorists loaded their cargo. Through the crack in the hatch Frank could see that they were hoisting steel drums into the hold—and he caught a glimpse of a radiation warning sticker on one of the barrels.

"How are we going to get out of here?" Richards asked in a hushed voice.

"We might get a chance to slip out after they finish loading," Frank said.

"That's not much of a plan," Richards said.

"We don't have much of a choice," Frank responded.

"That's the last of 'em," the mustached terrorist declared.

"Good," Bob replied. "Get our guest, and we'll be ready to roll."

Frank waited until he was fairly sure both men were out of the plane. Then he slowly pushed the hatch open to hear better.

"What's going on?" an angry voice snapped.

Frank froze.

"It's Vanessa!" Joe hissed.

"Where are you taking me?" Vanessa demanded.

"Shut up or I'll put the gag back on," the Assassin growled.

Joe heard Bob's cold laugh. "Relax and enjoy the flight, young lady. We'll be on our way shortly."

"Move the truck and open the hangar doors all the way," Bob ordered the other Assassin. "I'll radio the tower and get clearance for takeoff.

"In a few minutes this little game will be over," he crowed. "And the Assassins will be the winners!"

Chapter

16

THE TWIN OVERHEAD ENGINES roared, and the plane lumbered down the runway, a lethal cargo in its belly.

"We're taking off!" Richards hissed in alarm as the air-sea cargo plane shuddered and left the ground.

"You sure don't miss much, do you?" Joe muttered, wedged next to the writer in the cramped compartment. "How many Assassins are we up against?" Joe asked his brother.

"Only two, I think," Frank answered. "Bob and his cheerful friend with the mustache."

"There are three of us," Richards said. "Maybe we can overpower them." He paused and added, "Do you think they have guns?"

"They usually do," Frank responded, pushing the hatch open slightly. "So for now let's just assume they're armed to the teeth and crazy enough to open fire in a plane crammed full of radioactive waste containers."

"That sounds about right to me," Joe agreed. "What are you doing?" he asked as Frank pushed the hatch open a little wider and started to crawl out.

"They're all up in the cockpit," Frank said, "so I'm going to take a look at these barrels."

The cargo hold was almost as cramped as the baggage compartment. Frank counted a dozen steel drums. They were all plastered with radiation hazard warnings—and Frank quickly discovered that the red-and-white warning labels weren't the only items attached to each barrel.

"This could be a real problem," he murmured, carefully studying the bundle strapped onto the nearest container.

Joe and Richards crawled out to see what Frank had found.

"Plastic explosive," Frank explained, nodding to the grayish brown clump that might have been taken for a lump of clay, except for the wires sticking out of it. The wires snaked from the explosive charge to a small black box with a tiny antenna.

Frank pointed at the box. "This is the detonator. I'm pretty sure it's wired to be triggered by remote control."

Joe checked a few more of the barrels. "They're all rigged up just like that one," he reported.

Richards shuddered. "This whole plane is a gigantic toxic bomb!"

Frank studied the wiring on the explosive device. "I think I know how to disarm this gizmo."

Richards looked at him. "What if you're wrong?"

"Then I will have earned a valuable lesson, and I'll never make the same mistake again," Frank said, running his finger along one of the wires.

"There won't be enough of you left to make any kind of mistake again," Richards responded. "Did you think of that?"

"The thought crossed my mind," Frank said. "Do you have a better idea?"

"No," the writer admitted. He moved closer to Frank. "Explain what you're doing so I can help you disarm the rest of them."

"I'll keep watch in case we get uninvited company," Joe said. He snaked past the steel drums to the front of the cargo hold and crouched against the wall next to the cockpit door.

If anybody came through the door, Joe was in the best spot to get the drop on them. Frank knew his brother had another reason for positioning himself right outside that door. Vanessa was in the cockpit. Joe wanted to be as close to her as possible if things got rough.

When things get rough, Frank corrected himself. Even if he could disconnect all the bombs, they would still have to face the wrath of the Assassins.

Frank couldn't think about that now. He cleared his mind and focused on the explosive device in front of him. He took out his Swiss army knife and used the screwdriver blade to loosen the tiny screws on the faceplate of the detonator. Then he pried one end up a few inches and probed underneath with his finger.

When he was sure no wires were attached to the faceplate, Frank lifted it off and took a close look at the guts of the detonator.

"What do you think?" Richards asked, peering over Frank's shoulder.

"I think there are a lot of wires," Frank said.

"I noticed that," Richards said. "That's why I asked."

Frank slowly traced each of the wires, forming a diagram in his mind that he analyzed carefully. "This is the one," he finally announced, slowly spreading the tangle of wires and gingerly pinching a thin blue wire with his other hand.

Frank squeezed his eyes shut and tugged the wire gently. Nothing happened. Frank opened his eyes. The wire was still connected. Frank tugged a little harder. The wire didn't budge.

"Try this," Richards suggested, handing Frank the Swiss army knife that he had left lying on the deck. Instead of the screwdriver blade, he had extended the scissors attachment.

"Thanks," Frank said. He held his breath and snipped the blue wire, severing it neatly.

Nothing went boom, and all of Frank's limbs were still attached to his body. He remembered to breathe and let out a sigh of relief.

"Nice work," Richards congratulated him, patting Frank on the shoulder. "How did you figure it out?"

Frank shrugged. "Blue is my favorite color."

Richards stared at him. "You're kidding, right?"

Frank smiled cryptically. "I'll never tell."

Richards grinned back. "If we get out of this alive, it's going to make one terrific story."

Frank glanced around at all the barrels. "We still have a lot of work to do."

Frank worked quickly, moving from barrel to barrel.

"If we had another screwdriver," Richards said after Frank disarmed the seventh bomb, "I could help you finish this job faster."

"There are only a few barrels left," Frank responded. "And I have only one knife."

"Don't worry," Richard said. "I'll find something." He crawled off, and Frank moved to the next barrel.

Joe couldn't see what was going on, but he figured the absence of any thunderous explosion was probably a good sign. He was surprised when Richards's head suddenly popped up above the forest of steel drums. He seemed to be looking for something.

The writer's eyes found Joe, who used a silent hand gesture to tell him to get back down out of sight. Richards smiled and waved. Joe rolled his eyes and tried again.

Richards ignored him and kept looking around. The plane abruptly banked to one side. Richards stumbled and crashed into the wall. He reached out and grabbed a fire extinguisher.

The plane pitched the other way. Joe stifled a shout as the fire extinguisher came off the wall in Richards's hands. He lurched backward, frantically clutching the canister, and the fire extinguisher smacked into one of the steel drums with a heavy clang!

The cockpit door flew open, and the mustached terrorist burst into the cargo hold, brandishing a submachine gun. Joe threw his shoulder against the door, slamming it against the side of the Assassin's head. The man staggered and Joe lunged at him.

Joe and the snarling terrorist grappled for control of the gun, spun around, toppled over one of the barrels, then crashed onto the deck. There was a sickening thud, and the Assassin went limp. Joe stared at the man's slack face for a second and then looked up. Richards was standing over

the unconscious terrorist, ready to give him another whack on the head with the fire extinguisher if
he so much as twitched.

"Get the gun," Richards panted, brushing his
stringy hair out of his eyes.

"Let's not be hasty," a cold, measured voice
spoke up.

Joe turned around slowly. Bob was smiling at
him with an automatic pistol pressed against
Vanessa's skull. "Ah, Joseph," he said. "How
good it is to see you again." He glanced around
the cargo hold. "But where is your charming
brother?"

Joe shrugged. "He couldn't make it."

"What a pity," the Assassin said with a mock-
ing pout. "He'll miss the grand finale."

"You mean the part where you dump all this
toxic goop into the water supply?" Joe responded.

Bob chuckled. "That was a stroke of genius,
don't you think? While all those Network drones
were busy protecting their precious plutonium,
we walked off with enough radioactive material
to turn New York City into a wasteland!"

"Why are you doing this?" Richards asked.
"What do you hope to gain by poisoning millions
of people?"

"We *had* hoped to gain ten million dollars,"
Bob replied. "A cause such as ours requires sub-
stantial funds. The original plan was to deposit
the barrels in the reservoir and then make our

144

demands. Refusal to meet our terms would have resulted in unfortunate consequences."

He showed them the remote control switch he held in his other hand. "The radioactive waste in the barrels won't hurt anyone as long as it stays *in* the barrels. But if anything should happen to the barrels ..."

"Blackmail." Joe uttered the word with contempt.

The Assassin shrugged. "We prefer to think of it as negotiating from a position of strength. In any event, the situation has changed—and so have our plans."

"I don't suppose that means you've realized the error of your ways and want to turn over a new leaf," Joe said.

"I'm afraid not," Bob responded. His eyes were cold as he said, "Before you die, I want you to know that your meddling has forced us to take drastic measures."

"What does that mean?" Joe asked uneasily.

"We are circling over the reservoir on autopilot," Bob answered. He held up the remote control detonator switch. "When I push the button, the explosive charges on the barrels will rip this plane apart, and a thousand gallons of radioactive death will rain down into the water!"

"That's insane!" Richard blurted. "We'll all be vaporized in the blast—even you!"

"Yes, I know," Bob said, his eyes gleaming. "Isn't it glorious?"

"You're bluffing," Joe challenged, even though he could see that the man was deadly serious. He just wanted to keep him talking, anything to buy time. "Not even the Assassins would sink that low."

"You don't think so?" the terrorist said with a cold smile. "Let's find out."

Joe stared in horror, transfixed, as the Assassin pressed the detonator switch.

Chapter

17

JOE FELT HE WAS TRAPPED in a time warp nightmare as the grinning Assassin pressed the detonator switch. The bright red light on the remote control device taunted Joe as the device sent out the signal that would scatter them all across the sky in a cloud of radioactive dust.

If time had stopped, Joe wondered, why could he still hear the plane's twin engines droning steadily overhead and feel his heart pounding like a sledgehammer in his chest?

The Assassin's cruel grin wavered; doubt clouded his eyes, and the spell was broken. He scowled at the remote control and pressed the switch again and again. The winking red light was his only reward.

Joe realized the detonator was useless a split second before the terrorist did. Joe lunged at him while his attention was still focused on the device. Vanessa moved in the same instant. She knocked the pistol away from the side of her head and dove across the deck.

The Assassin snarled and swung the gun around. Joe slammed into him before he could take aim, driving him back through the cockpit door, sending them both crashing into the controls. The terrorist's head bashed against the instrument panel, shattering the glass faceplate on one of the gauges, and he slumped to the deck, out cold.

Joe staggered to his feet as the plane pitched down at a steep angle. He gaped out the windshield. The plane was tumbling out of the sky, hurtling toward the pristine waters of the manmade lake. Joe jumped into the pilot's seat. What he knew about flying wouldn't fill a Post-it note, but he knew that you had to pull back on the control yoke if you wanted the plane to go up. So he grabbed the yoke and yanked it as hard as he could.

The yoke fought back, refusing to budge. The muscles in Joe's arms and neck bulged as he strained to wrestle the plane out of the deadly dive. The surface of the reservoir loomed in the windshield. It seemed to be rushing up to greet the plane and wrap it in a dark, cold embrace. Joe knew the fate of countless innocent people was in his hands. If the plane crashed, the impact would rupture the barrels in the hold, spewing their lethal cargo into a water supply that reached into thousands of homes.

"Hang on!" Frank shouted, leaping into the co-pilot's seat and grabbing the other control yoke. "Keep pulling!" he rasped through clenched teeth, adding every ounce of his own strength to his brother's muscle power.

Joe felt the yoke start to yield under their combined effort. "It's working!" he gasped as the stiff controls slowly inched back.

The engines screamed, and the wind howled in the wings. The plane leveled off barely ten feet above the water. Joe could see ripples on the lake's surface, whipped up by the whirling turbulence of the propellers.

Joe slumped back in the pilot's seat and let Frank take over the controls. "Whew. That was close." He glanced over at his brother. "What took you so long?"

Frank smiled. "It took me a few seconds to pry my fingers off my knife. I was working on the last detonator when you ran out of snappy banter. When I realized Bob was going to hit the trigger, I made a blind stab. I still can't believe I cut the right wire."

"I know what you mean," Joe responded. "I still can't believe we're alive."

Frank's flying skills were stretched to the limit to land the cargo plane, but nobody ever knew how he sweated out the final approach. He took on the detached, casual air of the instructors who had trained him to fly smaller planes and made a smooth, flawless landing. When they were safely on the ground, Frank radioed the tower to send a message to the Network.

A short while later a horde of unmarked helicopters descended on the rural airport. Henkels personally supervised the transfer of the radioactive waste containers and the arrest of the two captured Assassins.

The Gray Man pulled the Hardys and Richards aside for a private talk.

"Let's be perfectly clear," the Gray Man said sternly. "None of this ever happened."

Joe shrugged. "I can live with that."

"Now, hold on a second," Richards responded indignantly. "This is hot stuff. You can't just put a lid on it."

Joe chuckled as he watched a team of Network agents load the steel drums with the radiation stickers into the helicopters. "We just risked our lives to make sure the lid didn't come off that particular batch of hot stuff."

"But this story will make a best-selling thril-